D0707980

HELPING HERCULES

PERSEUS

BELLEROPHON
& PEGASUS

HERCULES

ORPHEUS

Hi Hilary

HELPING
HERCULES

Francesca Simon

Francesca Simon
Illustrated by Tony Ross

MIDAS

PARIS

Orion
Children's Books

First published in Great Britain in 1999
as a Dolphin paperback
First published in Great Britain in this edition 2003
by Orion Children's Books
a division of the Orion Publishing Group Ltd
Orion House
5 Upper Saint Martin's Lane
London WC2H 9EA

Text © Francesca Simon 1997, 1999
Illustrations © Tony Ross 2003

A version of the title story was first published in *Timewatch*
(Dolphin, Quids for Kids) in 1997

ISBN 1 84255 248 1

The moral right of Francesca Simon and Tony Ross
to be identified as author and illustrator
of this work has been asserted.

All rights reserved. No part of this publication may be
reproduced, stored in a retrieval system, or transmitted, in
any form or by any means, electronic, mechanical,
photocopying, recording or otherwise, without the prior
permission of Orion Children's Books.

A catalogue record for this book is available
from the British Library.

Printed in Great Britain by
Clays Ltd, St Ives plc

For Adam Mars-Jones, just because

CONTENTS

1

HELPING
HERCULES

Susan was not what you would call helpful. Her parents nagged her to do more tidying but it did no good. In Susan's opinion, parents should do all the housework, leaving children free to enjoy themselves. She had far better things to do with *her* time then hoover the sitting room or dust the shelves.

Her parents, unfortunately, did not agree.

Every Sunday night her father handed out the weekly chores.

'Freddie, you empty the wastepaper baskets,' said Dad. (When Susan did it she made sure most of the rubbish ended up on the carpet.)

'Okay,' said Freddie, who was only five and got all the easy tasks.

'Eileen, you set and clear the table,' said Dad. (When Susan did it she always broke at least one plate and wiped all the crumbs straight on to the floor.)

'Sure,' said Eileen.

'Susan, you clean out the kitty litter tray,' said Dad.

'It's not fair! I always get the worst jobs!' said Susan.

'I cleaned the kitty litter last week,' said Eileen. 'Now it's your turn.'

'Everyone in this family has to help out,' said Dad.

'I'm far too busy and I'm not your slave,' snarled Susan. 'Clean it out yourself.'

She didn't even like the cat. Stinky's main pleasure in life was throwing up on the stairs and leaping onto laps with his claws out.

'SUSAN!' said Dad.

'I won't do it!' shrieked Susan. 'I hate this!'

'Go to your room,' said Dad. 'And don't come down until you're ready to help.'

Susan flounced upstairs and went into her bedroom, giving the door a good loud slam. Just in case the taskmasters downstairs hadn't heard, she opened her door and banged it shut again a few more times.

She'd show them. She'd starve before she came down and then they'd be sorry. She'd have a great time right here.

Susan looked around her messy room. She could play with her knights but she wasn't really in the mood, especially since that brat Freddie had snapped off all the horses' tails. She could practise her recorder ... no way. Her bossy parents liked hearing her play.

Then Susan saw the old cigar box tucked up on a high shelf. Aha! Her coin collection. She hadn't looked at it for ages, and she had that old Greek coin Uncle Martin had given her for her birthday.

Susan kicked her way through the dirty clothes, books and papers littering the floor, pulled her collection down from the shelf – knocking off a stack of books in the process – and got out her coin catalogue.

Then she unwrapped the precious coin. It had

belonged to her grandfather and great-grandfather before him, Uncle Martin had said. Now it was hers. 'We middle kids have to stick together,' he'd said, pressing the silver coin into her hand. 'Use it well.' Susan held the coin and looked at it carefully.

The coin was small and round, with worn, uneven edges. The front showed a man wearing a lionskin cloak and holding a ferocious boar. Well, that was easy enough, it was Hercules. She flipped it over. But instead of the head of a god or goddess, there were strange signs and carvings.

Susan opened her catalogue, and searched. She looked at every picture of the Ancient Greek coins and then looked again. Then she checked the Roman coins to see if it could be there, even though she knew perfectly well it was Greek. But there was no sign of this coin.

How odd. There were two possibilities here. One, that the coin was so rare – and so valuable – that it was not in her catalogue. The second possibility – no. That was too silly for words.

Susan sat on her bed and held the coin up to the light. Was her mind playing tricks, or did a strange, dull gleam come from Hercules' eyes? She turned the coin over in her fingers, feeling its worn surface. Was it her imagination, or did the coin feel warm?

Naturally, Susan did not believe in magic. Only little kids like Freddie believed in nonsense like flying carpets, magic lamps, and wishing wells.

'Okay coin, if you're magic, I wish . . .' Susan paused for a moment and closed her eyes, 'I wish that I could fly around the room.' She opened her eyes. She was still plonked on her bed.

'Ha,' said Susan.

'I wish,' said Susan, 'that everything on the floor would put itself away.'

She opened her eyes. Her bedroom was as big a pigsty as ever.

How silly I am, thought Susan. Then she looked at the coin, and smiled.

'I wish,' said Susan, closing her eyes and rubbing the coin between her fingers, 'that I could meet Hercules.'

Next moment the bed seemed to give way and she fell heavily to the ground. But instead of falling on the familiar grey carpet, she landed on a cold stone floor.

Susan blinked. Her bedroom was gone. She was in the corner of an immense room, with stone columns, walls black with smoke, embroidered hangings and flickering torches. Men lined the walls on either side, all standing to attention, their eyes fixed on a little man huddled against the back of a large throne.

In front of her towered a giant man, wearing a yellow lion skin tied over his shoulder and round his waist. The beast's fanged head glowered on top of his, like a bristling helmet. A great sword dangled by his side, and a quiver full of arrows hung from his shoulders. A huge olive-wood club lay beside him. In his arms the man held up a bellowing boar.

I must be dreaming, thought Susan.

Then the giant flung the frantic beast onto the floor. Its tied feet lashed the ground.

'Here's the Erymanthian boar, Eurystheus!' boomed Hercules, for of course it was he.

The little man leaped out of his throne and started howling.

'Get that thing out of here!' shrieked Eurystheus.

Then he scrambled into a large brass pot, screaming with terror.

'OUT! OUT! OUT!'

Hercules laughed, scooped up the writhing boar as if it were a bag of sugar, walked up to the open double doors and hurled the snorting boar through them. A few moments later Susan heard a gigantic splash.

I haven't got my wish, this is only a dream, thought Susan. No need to worry.

But just in case, she crept behind an urn.

Hercules stomped back into the room.

'Is that boar gone yet?' whimpered the voice from the brass pot.

'It's gone, you big coward,' sneered Hercules. 'I flung him into the sea. I'll bet it's halfway to Crete by now.'

Two fingers appeared on the top of the jar.

'Are you sure?' whined the king.

'YES,' snarled Hercules.

'Don't you ever bring any more wild animals to my palace again,' said Eurystheus, climbing back onto his throne. He smoothed his rumpled tunic and took hold again of his sceptre. The men lining the walls leaned forward, awaiting orders.

'Right Hercules, next labour,' said the king, and he started to giggle. 'It's the smelliest, stinkiest, most horrible job in the whole world and you'll never ever be able to do it! Killing the lion and the hydra and capturing the hind with the golden horns and that boar was nothing compared to this! You've heard of King Augeas at Elis and his three thousand cattle? Well, I order you to go and clean out his stables in one day. And better bring something to plug your nose — those stables haven't been cleaned for thirty years — ha ha ha!'

Hercules scowled but said nothing.

'Who's this?' said the king suddenly, pointing straight at Susan.

I'm out of here, thought Susan. She rubbed the coin, which she still had clutched in her hand, and wished frantically to be home.

Nothing happened.

Then strong arms grabbed her and pushed her before the king.

'Who are you?' demanded the king.

'I'm Susan,' said Susan, trying to stop her voice from shaking.

'Where are you from?'

'London,' said Susan.

'Never heard of it,' said the king. He looked at her more closely, and a big smile spread across his face.

'See this girl, Hercules?' said the king. 'You take her along to clean the stables. I'm sure she'll be a great help.'

'WHAT?' screamed Hercules.

'And mind you keep her alive – that's part of your labour, too,' said the king, rubbing his hands.

Hercules glared at Susan. She glared back at him. But before she could say anything he tucked her under his arm, strode out of the palace and started walking along the cliffs high above the choppy, wine–dark sea.

'Put me down!' ordered Susan. 'Put me down!'

Hercules ignored her.

'I can walk by myself, thank you very much,' said Susan.

'Listen, pipsqueak,' snapped Hercules. 'I don't like this any more than you do. But the sooner we get to King Augeas at Elis and muck out his filthy cattle the sooner you and I can go our separate ways.'

'I'm not helping you,' said Susan. 'I'm not your slave. Clean out your own stable.'

'Do you realize, brat, that I could crush you with my little toe?' said Hercules.

'You have to keep me alive – the king said so,' said Susan.

Hercules gnashed his teeth.

'I'm bigger than you, and you'll do what I say,' he growled.

'Bully!' said Susan.

Hercules twisted his thick neck and stared at her.

'Watch your tongue, you little worm,' said Hercules. 'I'm famous for my bad temper.'

'So am I,' said Susan.

'Oh yeah?' said Hercules.

'Yeah,' said Susan. 'When my sister Eileen squirted me with a water pistol I hit her. So go on, what's the worst thing you ever did?'

'When I was a boy my music teacher slapped me for playing a wrong note so I whacked him with my lyre and killed him,' said Hercules.

Susan gasped. That was pretty terrible. She didn't think hitting Eileen was quite on the same level.

'What a grump you are, Hercules,' said Susan.

Hercules gripped his great olive-wood club.

'You'd be grumpy too if you were a slave to a snivelling little toe-rag like Eurystheus and had to do whatever horrible job he set you.'

'Humph,' said Susan. 'So when do we get to the stables?'

'Soon,' said Hercules.

'How soon is soon?' said Susan. 'I have better things to do with my time than help *you*.'

'Be quiet,' said Hercules. 'And stop whining.'

On and on and on they travelled.

'Aren't we there yet?' Susan moaned for the hundredth time. Then she sniffed. The fresh smell of olive groves had suddenly changed into something less pleasant.

Hercules sniffed.

'Yup,' he said. 'We're getting near King Augeas' stables.'

A few more strides and the stink was overwhelming.

'Pooh,' said Susan. 'What a smell.'

'Pretty bad,' said Hercules grimly.

They walked in silence through the choking stench until they stood in the stable yard. Far off in the distance Susan could see thousands of cattle grazing in the fields between two rivers.

Susan stared at the huge stables. Never in her most horrible nightmares had she ever seen so much filth and dung. The sludgy, slimy, stinky mucky piles went on for miles.

And the smell – goodness gracious, it was awful!

Hercules looked glum.

'Right, to work,' he said.

'What's your plan?' asked Susan.

'Get that bucket and start shovelling. We'll heap all the muck out here.'

Susan gaped at him.

'*That's* your plan?' she said. 'We'll never finish in a day.'

'Shut up and start mucking out,' ordered Hercules.

Very very reluctantly, Susan got her bucket. Even more reluctantly, she picked up a shovel. Holding her nose with one hand, she approached the first reeking corner. Of all the magic adventures in the world, she got to clean out a stable.

'Yuck!' squealed Susan. She poked her shovel gingerly into the nearest cattle dung.

'Bleech!' She tossed the first noxious shovelful into the stableyard.

'Pooh! Ugh. Gross.' This was worse than cleaning out the kitty litter. This was a million billion trillion times worse than cleaning out the kitty litter. If she ever got back home she would never complain again.

Beside her, Hercules shovelled like a whirlwind, bending and hurling and twisting so fast she could hardly see him.

Half an hour passed.

'Right, ten stalls down, only 2,870 to go,' said Hercules.

'Actually, 2,990,' corrected Susan. 'At this rate, we'll be here five years. You're supposed to clean these stables in a day.'

'Just keep working,' snapped Hercules, digging ferociously. 'If you're so smart you come up with a better plan.'

Susan scowled. She could not bear the stench another second.

'Wait a minute,' said Susan. An idea had flashed into her head. She looked at Hercules.

'Just how strong are you?' she said.

Hercules went up to the thick stone wall at the side

of the stable building and punched a gaping hole into it with one swing of his club.

'THAT STRONG!' bellowed Hercules.

'Then listen,' said Susan. 'I've got a great idea. Remember those rivers we crossed coming here?'

'The Alpheus and the Peneus? So?'

'What if you dug a channel and diverted the rivers to run through the stables?' said Susan. 'The current would do the work for us and wash away all this muck. All you'd have to do is knock holes in the stable walls at either end, and then rebuild them once the stables were clean. Oh yes, and turn the rivers back to their original beds.'

Hercules stared at her.

'Hmmm,' he said. 'Hmmm,' he said again, grabbing his club and running off.

Soon Susan heard a shout.

'Watch out! Water's coming!'

Susan dashed into the fields, just in time to see a torrent of water pour into the stables.

In no time at all they were washed clean.

Susan cheered as she watched Hercules rebuild the walls and force the rivers back to their beds.

'That's that,' said Hercules, looking over the sparkling stables with satisfaction. 'Time for me to head back to that snivelling slave-driver. You're free to go, so bye bye.'

Go where, thought Susan frantically. She fumbled in her pocket and took out the coin.

'Wait. Look at this,' she said, handing it to Hercules.

He took the coin and stared at it. Slowly he turned it over and over.

'It's me,' he said at last. 'I'm famous. Of course my

muscles are much bigger than this picture shows but it's not bad. Don't I look handsome?'

'You look okay,' said Susan. 'Turn it over. What does that writing say?'

Hercules looked for a long time at the Greek letters. Had he killed his Greek teacher too, Susan wondered, before he'd learned to read?

'It says, ΤΙ ΕΤΗΕΛΕΙΣ – what do you wish?' he said at last.

'I wish to go home,' said Susan.

'So go,' said Hercules.

'I can't,' said Susan. 'I don't know how. I wished that before and it didn't happen.'

'That's how these magic things work,' said Hercules. 'You never quite know why or how. Let me try it. I wish a fountain would burst out of the ground when I stamp my foot.'

He stamped. The earth trembled, but no water appeared.

'See,' said Susan sadly, 'it's not very reliable. Can I have it back, please?'

'Sorry,' said Hercules, grinning stupidly at his carved picture. 'I'll keep this.'

'Give me back my coin!' shouted Susan.

'No,' said Hercules. 'Finders-keepers.'

'You didn't find it, I just showed it to you!' she screamed.

'Tough,' said Hercules.

Susan scowled at him.

'I need that coin to get home,' she said. 'Is this the thanks I get? Or do you want people to know that the great Hercules needed a girl's help to complete one of his labours?'

Hercules paused.

'All right,' he said. 'I'll give the coin back if you swear an oath you will keep your part in my labour a secret.'

'I swear,' said Susan.

'Swear by the River Styx, the black river of Hades,' said Hercules.

'I swear by the River Styx,' said Susan.

Hercules took one last look at his picture, then reluctantly gave her back the coin. Susan rubbed it between her fingers and wished.

At once Susan felt herself falling. But instead of landing in the dirt she found herself stretched out on her own soft bed.

Susan rubbed her head. She felt dizzy.

'Gosh, what a horrible dream,' said Susan, looking at the coin clasped tightly in her fist. She went to her bookshelf, took down her book of Greek myths and quickly read through Hercules' labours.

'What a creep!' she said. 'He *did* take all the credit for cleaning the stables. Hold on, I'm being silly,' she said, thumping herself. 'It was only a dream.'

She ran out of her bedroom.

'Mum, Dad, I'm ready to help now!' she shouted, clumping down the stairs. She paused at the kitchen door, where her family were eating dinner.

Everyone stared at her.

'What's wrong?' said Susan.

Eileen choked.

Stinky stalked out of the room.

Freddie held his nose.

'Pooh,' he said, waving his hand in front of his face.

'Where have you been?' said Dad. 'You smell like you've been living in a stable.'

2

OBLIGING
ORPHEUS

Susan hesitated. Should she tell them? But what could she say?

'We're waiting for an explanation,' said Dad.

'No big deal. I was helping clean out a stable,' muttered Susan.

'And who were you helping?' said Dad.

'Just someone,' said Susan.

'Who?' said Mum.

'His name's Hercules, all right?' snapped Susan.

'We don't know any Hercules,' said Eileen. 'What a funny name.'

Her mother sighed.

'What have we told you about fibbing, Susan?' she said sharply. 'When you tell silly stories no one will ever believe you when you tell the truth. There are no stables within miles of this house.'

'I *am* telling the truth,' said Susan. 'Uncle-' she was just about to mention Uncle Martin's magic coin when some instinct warned her to keep her mouth shut. If her parents confiscated the coin she would never have another adventure again.

'Uncle Martin will believe me,' she finished lamely.

'Just go upstairs and have a bath,' said Mum. 'And put those disgusting clothes straight in the washing machine.'

Susan stomped upstairs, jumbled her clothes into a heap and flung herself into the bath. She needed to think.

As far as she knew, you couldn't wind up smelly from a stable you'd visited in a dream. Therefore, incredible and unbelievable as it seemed, the coin had whirled her back to Ancient Greece.

But was that all it could do?

Susan reached for the coin.

'I wish for a million pounds,' she said.

Nothing happened. Perhaps she was being too greedy.

'I wish for one pound,' she said.

Still nothing happened.

'I wish for a chocolate biscuit,' said Susan.

Biscuitless, she placed the coin carefully on the floor.

Clearly, it wasn't a wishing coin, but a Greek time-travel coin.

I'm going to have fun, she thought, smiling and splashing bath water all over the floor.

SCREEECH! SCREEEEECH! SQUEEEAK!

It was three days later. Susan was practising her violin. She was trying to learn all the music she hadn't learned all week fifteen minutes before her lesson. This was not an easy task.

Freddie ran past holding his ears. Eileen dashed

24

downstairs to the kitchen and slammed the door. The neighbours closed their window. Even Stinky yowled.

Susan didn't feel like practising. She felt like screaming.

'Just do twenty minutes a day,' said her music teacher Mrs Parry. 'You'll play beautifully in no time.'

Huh, thought Susan. If I practised for twenty years it would make no difference. I'll still sound like a strangled grasshopper. Why she had switched from the recorder she would never know. She did know, actually. Her big sister Eileen played the recorder about a million times better than she did. Susan wanted to play an instrument that no one else in her family played. That way she could be the best. That was the theory, anyway.

She scraped her bow across the strings.

'Twinkle, twinkle – SQUEAK! Little – SCREEEEECH,' shrieked the violin. 'How I – SCREEECH – wonder – SCREECH – how you SCRAAAAATCH ...'

'Susan!' shouted her mother. 'Stop playing like that! It's time to go to your lesson.'

'It's no use!' screamed Susan. 'I hate the violin!'

In a fury she kicked the case. There was a rattling sound.

For a moment Susan couldn't think what it was, then she remembered. The Greek coin. The precious magic coin. She'd put it in her violin case to keep it safe.

'Come on Susan! Get down here! It's time for your lesson!'

'I wish I didn't have to go,' she muttered, plonking the violin in its case and slinging it across her shoulder. 'I wish I were anywhere but here.'

Susan's legs buckled beneath her as the silver-grey mist swirled round. She fell down, down, down …

Susan opened her eyes. The mist was gone. She shook her dizzy head. She was in a shady forest grove of ancient oaks. The air was hushed and still.

I'm not ready, thought Susan, feeling panicky. She wasn't in the mood for an adventure at all.

Then, in the distance, she heard music. The sweetest, most beautiful music she had ever heard. The music came closer and closer through the trees, a man's voice, singing. But where was it coming from? The skies? The earth? The plaintive, haunting melody swirled round her, sweet and sorrowful.

Susan found herself on her feet, dancing. As she raised her arms and twirled, she had the strangest feeling that around her the oaks danced, too, bending and swaying towards the music. There was a THUD THUD THUD as even the rocks appeared to leap from the ground.

It must be the wind, thought Susan. And then she saw that the great oaks circled round one another, forming the patterns of a stately dance. But so magical was the music that it did not seem strange. Even the pair of wolves crawling on their paws, whimpering, and the lion rolling on its back, its paws stroking the air, seemed somehow as it should be.

And then she saw him. A young man was playing and singing as he approached. What a voice! Tears filled her eyes. He held what looked like a small harp with two curved horns in his left hand, which he plucked while he sang his song of sorrow. Then he saw Susan. Instantly he stopped playing.

'The gods have answered my prayers! Nymph, nymph, help me! Help me!'

Susan looked around. They were alone in the grove. There was only the CLUMP! CLUMP! THUD! THUD! sound as the oaks stood fixed in their dancing circle, and the rocks lay still.

The man stared at her wildly and fell to his knees.

'I beg you, help me rescue my wife,' implored the singer.

'Me?' said Susan.

'Of course, you,' said the man.

'Where is she?'

The musician gulped. He glanced around to see if they were alone.

'The House of Hades,' he whispered.

Susan shivered. The very name sounded horrible. It did not sound like the sort of house it would be fun to visit. Where had she heard that name before?

'What's she doing there?' she asked.

'What do you think?' snapped the singer. 'Forgive me, nymph,' he added quickly. 'Grief has made me mad.'

A terrible memory flashed through Susan's mind.

'Hold on a minute,' said Susan. 'Isn't Hades where dead people go?'

'Shh! Don't speak that terrible word so loudly!' hissed the singer. 'Do you want to attract the attention of the King of the Underworld? Of course it's where dead spirits go,' he added. 'My Eurydice stepped on a poisonous snake running from that fiend Aristaeus, it bit her, and … and …' he broke off, gulping with sobs.

Suddenly Susan knew who he was.

'You're Orpheus the musician.'

'None other,' said Orpheus, sniffing. 'And are you a wood nymph, or a river nymph?'

Susan thought quickly. If she said she was a water nymph he might expect her to jump in some freezing pool.

'Wood nymph,' said Susan.

'Just like my Eurydice,' he said sadly. 'So you'll help me, then. I've got to get her back from the Underworld and I don't know how. What should I do?'

Orpheus looked at her helplessly.

'Uh,' said Susan. 'Look, I'm really sorry, but I'm not exactly sure how to, uh, bring people back from the dead. Even clever wood nymphs can't do that.'

'If you can't help me, then I am lost,' said Orpheus. He twanged a few melancholy notes. Lost … lost … echoed through the quiet grove and reverberated down the steep valley.

Suddenly Susan had an idea. 'Your playing …' she began. 'Wow. It's fantastic. Perhaps you could charm

Hades into letting her go, the way you've charmed the beasts and the trees.'

'Oh nymph, you are a genius,' shrieked Orpheus. 'Let's go, let's go at once.'

'Go where?' said Susan.

'The entrance to Hades' kingdom is at the great cave at Taenarum,' he said. 'It's just a short journey from here.'

Before Susan could say another word, Orpheus had seized her arm and they were off.

I'm in for it now, thought Susan, as they trudged along narrow hillside paths scented with the smell of lemons. Me and my big mouth.

'What's that you're carrying?' asked Orpheus.

Susan had forgotten about her violin.

'My violin,' said Susan.

'What's that?' asked Orpheus.

'It's a musical instrument,' she said, seeing his puzzled look.

'Ah,' said Orpheus. 'Perhaps you will lighten our weary path and play as we walk.'

'I don't think that's a very good idea,' said Susan quickly.

'Don't be modest, nymph,' said Orpheus. 'It would give me great pleasure to hear you play.'

That's what you think, thought Susan grimly. This was worse than she could ever have imagined. It was bad enough playing for Mrs Parry. Now she had to play for Orpheus, the greatest musician who ever lived.

Slowly she opened the violin case. There was the coin, glowing faintly. There was now a lyre on its front. Susan picked up the coin and wished that she could play beautifully. The magic owed her that much. Then she popped the coin in her pocket, and tucked the violin under her chin. Orpheus looked at her, beaming. Oh please, magic, do your stuff, she thought.

Then Susan started to play. Trees flung back their branches. Angry growls came from the bushes.

Orpheus covered his ears.

'By the gods, what a sound,' he said.

Susan blushed bright red. That rotten, horrible coin has let me down, she thought.

'Told you I couldn't play,' she snapped.

'I am not familiar with your instrument,' said Orpheus kindly. 'May I try it?'

Susan handed him the violin. 'Go ahead.'

Orpheus stroked the wood, and dangled the bow from his left fingers.

'Hold the bow in your right hand,' muttered Susan.

'Ah,' said Orpheus. Then he raised the bow to the strings and began to play.

His fingers darted up and down the keyboard, his bow sailed across the strings.

Susan could not believe her ears. How did the

wooden box which sounded so scratchy under her fingers give forth such magic under his?

'How do you do that?' she asked.

'It is my gift,' said Orpheus simply.

They walked in silence down into a barren valley, bordered by bare, steep cliffs. Susan noticed there was no sound – even the birds were silent.

'We're here,' said Orpheus quietly, standing in front of a narrow opening in the cliffside, partly blocked by a heavy boulder.

'This is Taenarum, the entrance to Hades,' he said. 'Are you brave enough to enter?'

'Of course I am,' said Susan, while inside her a voice screamed, No you aren't! Get out of there while the going's good!

Orpheus strummed on his lyre, and the giant boulder heaved itself aside.

'Actually I'm late for my violin lesson,' said Susan. 'Perhaps another time.' But Orpheus had already disappeared inside. Susan hesitated for a moment. I don't suppose there's any point in wishing I wasn't here, she thought, closing her eyes. Then she opened them again. The entrance to the Underworld was still there.

'Nymph, where are you?' came a panicky-sounding voice from inside the mountain.

Susan squared her shoulders, and followed Orpheus down inside the earth.

BUMP! In the darkness Susan collided with him.

'Hey!' she snapped. 'Watch where you're going!'

Orpheus muttered something under his breath.

'What?' said Susan.

'Would you walk first? I'm scared of the dark,' murmured Orpheus.

31

'Now you tell me!' said Susan. She didn't like the dark much either, if truth be told.

'All right,' she said.

'Thank you, nymph,' said Orpheus humbly. 'If you don't mind I'll just hang on to your tunic.'

Down, down, down they descended into the pit. At times the path widened and they scrambled across dark valleys, then down, down, down through the narrow, twisting tunnels of the Underworld. The air was dank and musty, the darkness terrible. Her violin case clunked against her back. Susan resisted the urge to pitch it into the abyss.

Just when Susan thought her aching feet could not walk another step, they reached the misty shores of the black river, Styx. Across its still, stagnant waters, a ferryman sat, head bowed.

'You get his attention,' whispered Orpheus. 'My courage is failing.'

'Why me?' said Susan.

Orpheus turned pleading eyes on her. 'You do the talking, I'll do the playing.'

Susan sighed.

'Yo! Ferryman!' she called. Her voice reverberated across the swamp, a shrill, thin echo.

The old man looked up. He seemed so shocked that for a moment Susan thought he was going to topple backwards out of his black boat. Then he spat, dipped his oars and rowed close to them.

'And where do you think you're going?' snarled the man. 'Yes, you two, in the bodies. This is a place for dead people only.'

'We've come to fetch his wife, Eurydice. She shouldn't be here,' said Susan.

The ferryman laughed and rowed a little closer.

'That's what they all say. Only the dead can cross this river, mortals. And even if I did row you across, which I won't, no matter how many obols you've got under your tongue, that watchdog with the three heads and the fangs will soon stop you sneaking through the gates. So scram.' He snorted and turned away.

'There's no need to be so rude,' said Susan.

The slap-slap of the oars on the water was her only reply.

She turned to Orpheus, who appeared transfixed by the fast-disappearing ferryman.

'Play!' hissed Susan.

Orpheus shook himself and raised his lyre. The song of sadness filled the misty air. Slowly, the boat drew closer to them until its tip touched the boggy shore. Orpheus, still playing, climbed aboard. Susan followed.

They rowed across the steaming, sulphurous river, between sheer black walls. All around were moans and sighs, as the souls of the dead reached out across the water. The foul stink of pitch and gas and sulphur stung their nostrils.

As they left the boat, a terrible howl echoed across

the dripping black walls. Susan shivered.

Then a monstrous three-headed hell-hound loomed up, lashing its snake tail, with serpent heads writhing all over its back. The beast towered above them, snarling and snapping, its cruel jaws dripping with foam.

'What's that?' gasped Susan.

'Cerberus, who guards the gate,' said Orpheus, ducking behind Susan. He looked pale.

'Go on, sing!' said Susan.

Slowly Orpheus raised his lyre.

'Hurry! Before he eats us both!' screamed Susan.

Cerberus, bellowing, stalked towards them. Orpheus froze.

'Help!' he squeaked.

'Play! Play!' she urged.

'Plink! Plink!' came the pitiful sound from Orpheus' lyre. Then he opened his mouth to sing. A hoarse whisper came out.

'What's wrong?' shouted Susan as Cerberus advanced, snarling, the snakes hissing and twisting on his back.

'I can't. I'm scared of dogs. You play!' gasped Orpheus.

There was no time to argue. Cerberus was now so close Susan could smell the foul breath pouring out of his three slavering jaws.

Hands trembling, Susan got out her violin. I swear I'll practise more if I come out of here alive, she vowed, grabbing the bow.

'Twinkle – SHRIEK – twinkle, little star – SCRATCH!

How I wonder what you are,' yowled the violin.

For a moment Cerberus stopped barking.

'Carry on,' whispered Orpheus.

Susan played on. Then Cerberus, standing still, started snarling again.

They took one step closer to the gate.

The monster's yowls changed. Each head started howling in time to Susan's playing.

TWINKLE

AWHOOOOOOOAWHOOOAWHOOO

TWINKLE

AWHOOOOOOOAWHOOOOOOAWHOOOOOO

LITTLE

AWHOOOOOOOAWHOOOOOOO
AWHOOOOO

STAR

AWHOOOOOOOAWHOOOOOOO
AWHOOOOO

Closer and closer they got to the gate. Cerberus sank to the ground, howling happily.

'What's that horrible racket?' snapped Tantalus, pausing for a moment from reaching for a pear that dangled just out of reach.

Sisyphus looked so stunned that he stopped pushing his stone up the hill.

'What's this, some new torment for me?' he shouted as the rolling stone knocked him backwards.

Then Susan and Orpheus were through the black gates. Behind them Cerberus whimpered sadly.

'Well done,' said Orpheus.

Susan glowed. Not many musicians could say they'd been complimented by the greatest player of all.

Ahead, through the gloom and the shadowy shapes billowing aimlessly around them, Susan saw a towering black palace. Trembling, she and Orpheus walked through the marble doors and into the vast throne room, where the King and Queen of the Underworld sat in stony silence.

The grim king rose as they approached.

'How dare the living pollute our land with their hot stench,' he boomed.

'What cheek!' agreed his grey queen, Persephone, her cold eyes raking them.

Susan grabbed Orpheus.

'If you love her, play! Play!' she hissed. 'Play as you've never played in your life.'

And Orpheus played. He sang of his sorrow, his loneliness, and his love. He sang of Eurydice, her beauty, her youth, their short time together before the cruel snake tore them apart.

Hades curled up on his throne and cried.

Persephone cried. Susan cried. And still Orpheus played till it seemed that the walls would melt with the beauty and the sorrow of his music.

Finally the king wiped his eyes. He gazed for a moment at the unfamiliar tears staining his fingers, then looked at Orpheus.

'It is forbidden for the dead to return to the Upper World,' he said softly. 'But you have melted my heart with your song. Return to the living. Eurydice will follow. But I make one condition –'

'Anything!' shouted Orpheus.

'That you promise not to look at her until you reach sunlight. If you do, she will be lost to you for ever.'

'Thank you, thank you,' murmured Orpheus.

The queen looked at Susan. 'Is *that* what women are

wearing now in the Upper World?' she asked, eyeing Susan's clothes with distaste.

'Yes,' said Susan. 'And a lot more comfortable than dragging about in some old tunic,' she added.

'Humph,' said the queen.

Hades waved them away.

'Go now, and your Eurydice will follow.'

'Why'd you let them go?' demanded the queen. 'We could have had that music here for ever.'

'All in good time,' snapped the king.

Orpheus picked up his lyre and played as he and Susan walked quickly down the dank corridor, the very statues turning their heads to listen. Behind them Susan heard the faint rustle of a woman's long robe.

'Oh Zeus, is it her?' murmured Orpheus.

'Don't look,' said Susan. 'Keep playing.'

Out through the high gates they went, to the banks of the River Styx.

'You again,' said the ferryman, as he rowed them across.

'Is she with us?' asked Orpheus.

'That would be telling,' sniffed the ferryman.

Out of the boat they clambered, one, two, three.

'I can't bear this,' said Orpheus.

'You must,' said Susan. It was everything she could do not to look as well. Hades hadn't mentioned her, but better safe than sorry, she thought.

Up, up, up they climbed, towards the Upper World.

Gradually the light changed from black to grey.

'We're almost there!' shouted Susan. She started to run. 'I can see light up ahead!'

'Eurydice! We're almost there!' shouted Orpheus, hoarse but exultant.

There was no reply.

'Nymph! Why isn't she answering?' said Orpheus.

'I don't know,' said Susan.

'What if she isn't there?' said Orpheus. 'What if ...
Eurydice! Eurydice!' he called.

Still she did not answer.

And then Orpheus, at the very entrance to Hades,
turned his head, just a quick peek.

She was there, just behind him.

'Eurydice!' he murmured.

A whirlwind blew through the tunnel.

'Orpheuuuuus!' she wailed, as she tumbled into the
darkness. 'Orpheuuuuuus!'

'What have I done?' said Orpheus. 'What have I
done?'

'How could you!' shrieked Susan. 'Why did you look? I told you not to look!'

Orpheus let out a howl of despair.

'I was afraid she wasn't there,' he sobbed.

Susan burst into tears.

'I can't bear this,' she wept. 'I want to go home.'

'Home,' muttered Orpheus in a daze. 'Home. I shall go back to Thrace.'

And then Susan felt herself falling.

'Susan! I'm waiting!'

Susan shook herself. She was lying in a crumpled heap on her bedroom floor.

She was back.

'Coming, Mum,' said Susan, wiping the tears from her face.

Mrs Parry stared at her as she put down her bow.

'Goodness, you've improved!' she said. 'That was wonderful. I don't recognize your playing at all!'

'I had a good teacher,' said Susan.

3

PERSUADING
PARIS

'Now let me see,' said Mrs Winter, 'who shall I choose to play the queen?'

Susan's hand shot up. So did the hand of every other girl in the class. Even Big Bob waved his hand about, shrieking, 'Me! Me!'

Oh please pick me, thought Susan, shoving her hand in the air as high as it would go. She loved acting, and this year's class play promised to be such fun. The queen got to sword-fight, fly, *and* boss around loads of servants. She could see herself now, snapping her fingers at sluggish slaves with one hand while fighting off baddies with the other.

Mrs Winter's eyes swept over the class. Then she smiled.

'I think Helen should be the queen,' she said.

Helen smirked.

Susan groaned and slumped on the carpet. Stupid, stuck-up, bossy Helen. How *could* Mrs Winter make such a bad choice? She'd always liked Mrs Winter up till now, but never again. She was the nastiest, meanest, stupidest teacher in the world and she hated her.

'Sit up please, Susan,' said Mrs Winter.

Susan scowled and straightened up a fraction of an inch.

'Yasmin, you will be the evil wizard, Joshua, the magician, and the rest of you will be palace guards and servants,' continued Mrs Winter. 'Now, any volunteers for programme-makers and scene changers?'

Worse and worse, thought Susan sullenly, slumping down again. She did not want to play a servant. Phooey to that. She wanted to be the queen. Watching that horrible Helen tossing her curls and grinning triumphantly was unbearable.

'I'd be a much better queen than Helen,' Susan muttered. 'I'm a better actor, and I can sword-fight. Bet she can't.'

She glared at Helen and stuck out her tongue.

Helen stuck out her tongue back.

'Helen!' said Mrs Winter. 'Is that any way for a queen to behave?' Susan's heart leaped. Maybe Mrs Winter wouldn't let Helen play the queen after all. But Mrs Winter carried on chattering about props and costumes.

Susan reached into her pocket and took out her Greek coin, turning its warm, rough surface over and over in her fingers. She peeked at it under the table. Instead of a lyre the front now had a profile of a beautiful woman, her hair piled high. Susan's fingers tingled.

'Susan!' said Mrs Winter. 'You're away with the fairies! Kindly rejoin us and pay attention.'

Susan scowled and clutched the coin. 'I'll give you

away with the fairies,' she muttered, then closed her
eyes and wished.

'MOO!'
 'MOO!'
Susan looked up. She was lying on rough grass,
surrounded by cows. Their huge brown eyes were
staring down at her.
Susan waved her hands, and sat up.
'Shoo!'
The beasts took several steps back, then stood still,
their tails flicking at the flies buzzing about them.
She was in a sloping, hilly pasture, near the top of a
rocky mountain, surrounded by oak woods and the
jutting peaks of nearby hills, thick with black cypresses.
The hot sun blazed down from the cloudless blue sky.

Then Susan heard running footsteps, and a young, tall, very handsome herdsman came into view. The cows scattered as he approached. He saw her, then instantly stopped short, shading his eyes as if he were blinded by a brilliant light.

'Oh mighty and exalted goddess, shield my mortal eyes from your heavenly radiance!' cried the herdsman, flinging himself to the ground before her, narrowly missing several cowpats.

At last, someone who appreciated her, thought Susan, preening. And, a promotion from nymph to goddess! How thoughtful of the magic. She beamed at the handsome, prostrate herdsman.

'Where am I?' said Susan.

'On the highest peak of Mount Ida, oh noble and powerful one.'

'Ah,' said Susan, wishing she'd paid more attention in her geography lessons. 'And who are you, mortal?'

'I am Paris, a herdsman of Troy,' said the man. 'You've come for the beauty contest, I presume,' he added, continuing to hide his eyes. 'Forgive my blindness, but which goddess are you?'

Beauty contest? What on earth was he on about, wondered Susan. Unless, of course, freckles and wiggly teeth like hers were the height of Greek beauty.

'I am the goddess Susan,' she said majestically. 'The Fierce and Fair.'

Cautiously, the herdsman peeped through his fingers. He seemed to see her properly for the first time.

'The goddess ... Susan? Your fame has not yet travelled to this lonely place,' he said carefully. 'Where are the others?'

'What others?' said Susan.

'I was told to expect three: Hera, Heaven's queen, Athena, goddess of wisdom, and Aphrodite, goddess of love,' said Paris. 'There was no mention of a Susan. I naturally thought, given your sudden arrival in this lonely place, that you were the first. Although ... ' he looked at Susan more closely.

'Forgive me, you do seem a little, uh, small, for a goddess,' he said. 'You are a goddess from far away?'

'Yes,' said Susan. She thought quickly. 'Goddess of London. I've come to help you.'

Paris brightened at once.

'I'm glad you're here. I'm in the most terrible muddle. The messenger god Hermes came to see me and said I have to judge who is the most beautiful: Hera, Athena, or Aphrodite. It seems there was this wedding between King Peleus of Pythia and a sea nymph, Thetis, and naturally Eris the goddess of Strife wasn't invited, so during the wedding feast she sneaked in and threw a golden apple right in the middle of the guests. Look, here it is.'

Paris reached inside his roughly-woven tunic and brought out a glowing golden apple.

Susan took it, rolling its beautiful smooth surface between her hands. On it was written an inscription.

'What does it say?' she asked.

'For the fairest,' he said. 'That's why the goddesses all started quarrelling, and now by order of Almighty

45

Zeus I'm to pick the most beautiful.'

Susan stroked the shiny apple. How lovely it was. She longed to keep it.

'Why do you think Zeus wanted *you* to judge? Why didn't he just do it himself?'

'Because I'm so clever and good-looking,' said Paris, plucking the apple out of Susan's reluctant hands. 'Hermes did happen to mention that the gods consider me the handsomest man in the world.'

'I don't think so,' said Susan thoughtfully.

'Huh,' said Paris, looking offended.

'I mean you are perfectly handsome–' goodness these Greeks were vain! 'I think you were asked because Zeus didn't want to choose himself and have two enemies for life.'

'Ahh,' said Paris. 'I hadn't thought of that.' He frowned at the gleaming apple. 'Perhaps that's why my wife Oenone has been crying since I told her of Hermes' visit.'

Suddenly the meadow filled with light. Birds burst into song and the soft air was fragrant with perfume.

'By Hercules,' murmured Paris. 'Look at them.'

Susan shaded her eyes as the goddesses approached, tall, majestic, glorious. Their bare feet hardly touched the grass.

'Don't be frightened, mortal,' said the grey-eyed goddess, Athena, taking off her helmet and scattering her silky hair.

'Who is this ... person with you, who dares to look upon us?' demanded Hera.

'I am the goddess Susan of London, a powerful place far far away,' said Susan. 'I am famous there for ... for my beautiful feet and bad temper.'

Everyone stared at her grubby trainers.

'It's just a child,' said Athena. 'Leave her be.'

'You'll be quiet if you know what's good for you,' said Hera. Then she addressed herself to Paris.

'We want this to be a fair contest,' said Hera.

'Absolutely,' said Athena.

'Definitely,' said Aphrodite. She gave Paris a little wave. Athena glared at her.

'Paris, you just look us over and decide who is the fairest,' said Hera. 'Though I have no doubt one look at me will be enough to cast my rivals entirely in the shade. In fact, they might prefer to stand back a bit, lest my beauty show off their, ahem, blemishes.'

'Yes, and your gi-normous hips and chipmunk cheeks!' sneered Aphrodite.

'And your owl face!' growled Athena.

'Mule!'

'Crow!'

'Flea-bag!'

'Goddesses!' shouted Susan. 'Behave yourselves!'

The goddesses turned upon Susan.

'What did you say?' muttered Hera, raising her arm.

Suddenly Paris thrust the golden apple in Susan's hand. 'You choose,' he said.

'No way,' said Susan, thrusting it back. 'You're the judge.'

'You judge,' said Paris.

He passed the apple to her.

'You!'

'You!'

'All right,' said Susan, taking the apple and sighing loudly. What a fuss they were making over a silly contest. She gave the sulky goddesses a good look over.

'I object,' said Hera majestically.

'Paris can do as he likes,' simpered Aphrodite.

'Let's await the decision before we act in haste,' said Athena.

'Okay,' said Susan, 'I rule that since you are all equally lovely we split the apple three ways.' Now that *was* fair, she thought, and would stop a lot of bother and squabble.

For a moment the goddesses were silent. Then with one voice they turned on Susan.

'How dare you!' snapped Hera, her eyes darting fire.

'The idea,' said Athena, 'As if my beauty could be considered *equal* to those ... those ... hussies.'

Aphrodite tossed her head. 'Really, I've never heard anything so silly in my life. Perhaps, on a dark night, wearing veils, those two dishcloths might be mistaken for beauties. But to think that I, the loveliest goddess in the world, should merely be their equal – humph.'

'Turn her into a mouse!' screamed Hera.

'No, a spider!' shouted Athena.

'A worm!' hissed Aphrodite.

'Wait! Wait!' shouted Susan.

'WE WANT PARIS TO JUDGE!' shrieked the goddesses in unison.

'Great idea,' said Susan, handing the apple back to Paris and folding her arms. Those ungrateful goddesses.

Paris turned helpless eyes to her.

'Sorry, I tried,' she whispered.

Hera turned to Paris and spoke in a soft voice.

'Now we're just going to stand here quietly, not saying a word, and you'll judge who is the loveliest.'

'Agreed,' said Athena and Aphrodite.

Paris stood still for several moments, looking at first one and then the others, bouncing the apple up and down in his hand.

'Of course,' said Hera, 'should you choose me, I'll make you the most powerful man in the world. Your armies will conquer wherever they go and your fame will echo everywhere. Just think, mortal, power over all!'

'You're trying to bribe him,' said Susan. 'That's not fair!'

Everyone ignored her.

'Ooh,' said Paris. He walked towards Hera, the apple in his outstretched hand.

'Not so fast, young man,' said Athena, stepping forward and gazing at him with her sword-grey eyes. 'Choose me and I will give you the most precious gift of all – wisdom. You will be the wisest man alive, with unrivalled knowledge of men and women, the arts, and of yourself. With wisdom like yours everything will be possible.'

49

'Ooh,' said Paris. He walked towards Athena.

'Good choice, Paris,' said Susan. Lucky Greek. She'd *love* to be the wisest woman in the world. Why hadn't they offered bribes when *she* was judging? she thought indignantly.

Athena had her hand outstretched to take the prize when Aphrodite stepped forward, laughing.

'Paris, you big silly,' she giggled, tossing her long golden curls. 'A mortal's life is short, so why not spend it enjoying the love of the most beautiful woman in the world, Helen of Sparta? She is Zeus' daughter, and almost my equal for beauty and allure. Give me the prize and Helen will be yours.'

Paris stood still.

Susan grabbed his arm. 'You've already got a perfectly good wife, Paris!' she hissed. 'If you must choose, choose wisdom!'

'Shh,' said Paris. He looked as if he were hypnotized.

'Tell me more,' he said to Aphrodite.

She smiled her wonderful smile.

'Helen rules in Sparta with her husband King Menelaus,' said Aphrodite. 'But don't worry, I'll arrange everything.'

And she smiled again, shaking back her luxurious hair.

Susan was disgusted. Well, if they could all offer bribes for the apple, why shouldn't she?

'Power!' said Hera.

'Wisdom!' said Athena.

'Love,' breathed Aphrodite.

'Bubble gum!' said Susan.

Paris stopped.

'I thought you were told to be silent,' snapped Hera.

'What's bubble gum?' said Paris.

'It's the greatest,' said Susan, fishing about in her pocket and taking out a piece. 'Look, you pop it in your mouth like this–' in went the pink gum–' chew it about like this–' Susan's jaws worked vigorously at the gum, 'then, blow!'

Susan blew and blew and blew. The thin pink bubble round her face grew larger, and larger, and larger ... Then POP! The bubble burst.

The goddesses jumped in surprise and took a step back.

'Ooh,' said Paris. 'Magic.'

Susan slurped the gum back into her mouth. 'Bubble gum can't be beat,' she said.

Paris approached her.

'Could I have some?' he asked.

'Sure,' said Susan. She dangled a piece in front of him.

'I pronounce Susan the fairest,' said Paris, handing her the golden apple.

'WHAT?' shrieked the goddesses. Their faces went pale and then dark with rage.

'Yippee!' shouted Susan. She tossed Paris the pack of gum. He held it reverently in his hand while Susan cavorted gleefully, clutching the glowing apple and feeling its maddening power seep inside her as she did her victory dance, oblivious to everything save the thrill of her triumph. She, Susan, had been judged more beautiful than Hera, Athena, and Aphrodite!

'Nah nah ne nah nah, I'm the fairest of all!' she trilled.

'I'll show you the fairest, presumptuous brat!'

howled Hera, pointing her finger at Susan.

Susan shuddered.

She felt her body shrinking and curling, her face narrowing to a point. Fur sprouted and covered her. The apple thudded to the ground as her hands became tiny paws and she collapsed onto all fours. Her clothes slid off her into a heap.

'Wh-what's happening to me?' she said, but all that came out of her whiskered mouth was a squeak.

'There, mouse, now see who you will tell of your victory!' cackled Hera as Susan scrabbled about on the rocky ground, trying to avoid the gigantic pounding hooves of the frightened cows. 'To the crows!'

Keep calm, thought Susan. Keep calm, she repeated, as she heard Hera's voice boom:

'Now, Paris, you will judge once and for all who is *truly* the fairest.'

I must find the coin, thought Susan desperately. Her tiny feet pattered amidst the pebbles, rough grass, and daisies as she darted frantically about her clothes. Finally she nosed her way into the deep dark cavern of one pocket, and then the other.

Empty.

It must have fallen out, she thought miserably, as she wriggled free. Above her a hawk circled.

As if in a dream she heard Paris pronounce Aphrodite the victor, heard her silvery laugh, and saw the two rejected goddesses link arms and turn away.

Oh no! They were heading towards her.

Something glinted in the sunlight.

Susan leaped on it.

'Stop her!' cried Hera, looming up and blocking out the sun. Susan curled her paws tightly about the coin and wished with all her might.

Thirty pairs of eyes stared at Susan.

Mrs Winter opened her mouth and then closed it.

'What are you all looking at?' said Susan. She tried to stop panting. How wonderful it was to be back, in human form, sitting on the carpet.

Mrs Winter blinked. Then she shook her head.

'Uhm, right,' she said uncertainly. 'For a moment, Susan, I thought you were ... never mind.'

4

PARKING
PEGASUS

'Neigh! Neigh!'

'Shut up, Eileen!' bellowed Susan.

'NEIGH!! NEIGH!!' whinnied Eileen, louder than before, stomping on the ground and cantering madly up and down the field tossing her hair.

Susan's big sister Eileen was horse-mad. Pictures of horses plastered her walls. Pony stories cluttered her shelves. Riding ribbons dangled from every surface.

Susan hated horses.

Ughh, she shuddered, just thinking about them gave her the creeps. What could be more boring than spending your life bobbing up and down on some smelly old nag, and then wasting whatever time was left cleaning hooves and mucking out stalls? Susan had had quite enough mucking out in her adventure with Hercules to last her a lifetime, thank you very much.

And now her mother was insisting that she have riding lessons.

'Just one, to try it,' said Mum.

'I don't want to have riding lessons,' said Susan.

'What if I fall? What if the horse runs away with me? What if –'

'Oh do stop moaning, Susan,' snapped her mother. 'When I think what I would have given to have had riding lessons when I was a girl...' she sighed deeply.

'Scaredy-cat,' sniggered Eileen.

'Am not!' Susan flared.

'Then why not have a go?' said Eileen.

Susan felt like screaming. Why wouldn't they leave her alone? The truth was, horses terrified her. They were so big and moved so fast, and the thought of having to get on one was absolutely horrible. Almost as horrible as being turned into a mouse by Hera.

Susan had not had a magic adventure for weeks now.

That close call with the goddesses had frightened her. And then the coin playing that mean trick on her, returning her to Mrs Winter's class a moment before she'd got her right body back. Mrs Winter kept giving her strange looks and muttering about early retirement, while a few of her bolder classmates had even squeaked at her once or twice. That coin was cantankerous and untrustworthy, and Susan had firmly resolved to leave it alone.

In recent days, however, she'd found herself taking quick peeks at it. She could have sworn she had felt the coin beckoning to her from its hiding place in the little box, tucked inside an old purple sock. Susan had taken it out, felt its strange warmth, then quickly replaced it in her drawer. But this morning she'd decided to put it back in her pocket. Just for safe-keeping. Her little brother Freddie was always poking his nose into places where he wasn't wanted, and Susan was scared that he might find the magic coin.

Better to take it with her instead. After all, no harm in that. She and magic were through.

Now here she was, at a stable, face to face with a ferocious, furious, frisky mare that somehow she was expected to climb on and ride.

'No way,' said Susan, backing off.

'Don't be scared,' said the riding teacher. 'Nellie is as gentle as a little lamb. Put these sugar cubes in your pocket – you can give them to her after the lesson.'

Yeah, some lamb, thought Susan, gazing nervously at Nellie's big teeth and pounding hooves.

'Up you get,' said the instructor, heaving the quaking Susan into the saddle.

'Ahhh, ahhh, help!' squeaked Susan, swaying terrifyingly high above the ground.

'Feet in the stirrups, that's right,' said the instructor, adjusting the straps, 'and hold the reins like this, then–'

Afterwards, no one could say for sure what had happened. Suddenly Nellie snorted, and trotted off.

'AAAH,' screamed Susan. 'Help! Get me out of here!'

I shouldn't have said that, she thought, as the grey mist swept her up and whirled her away.

THUD!

'Ow!' said Susan loudly, as the magic belly-flopped her roughly onto the ground. You'd think the coin was punishing me for not using it, she thought crossly, sitting up and dusting herself off.

'Quiet, would you?' hissed a young man hiding behind a nearby rock. Susan jumped in surprise.

'And keep your head down. I don't want to scare him.'

'Scare who?' said Susan. They appeared to be alone near a clear, bubbling spring. The early morning sky was rosy-grey.

The young man didn't answer.

He was lying flat on his stomach in the sweet-smelling grass. In one hand he held a glowing golden bridle. The only sound was the harsh humming of the cicadas.

They lay there for a moment in silence.

'What *are* you doing?' said Susan.

'Shh, I'm waiting, can't you see? Now run along. Unless of course you've come from Athena to help me,' he added.

'Naturally,' said Susan grandly. 'I am the nymph, Susan. Who are you, and what needs doing?'

'I'm Bellerophon, and I've been trying for ages to capture the winged horse, Pegasus,' he whispered. 'Pegasus is the child of Poseidon and the monster Medusa. He's wild, roaming the sky and the land, and will allow no one near him. I have tried and tried and tried to catch him, without success, but fortunately the gods love me. I slept one night at Athena's temple and dreamed that she gave me a magic gold bridle and that Pegasus drank here at Pirene, in Corinth. When I woke, this bridle was in my hand.'

'Why are you so keen to capture him?' asked Susan.

'Because King Iobates has asked me to kill the fire-breathing monster Chimaera,' said Bellerophon. 'A truly fearsome beast, with a lion's head, goat's body and dragon's tail. I can't fight her without Pegasus. Shh, look.'

Bellerophon pointed to the pinkish sky. There was a whirr and flutter of wings and down from the dawn

sky flew a magnificent white horse. Susan's jaw
dropped. Open-mouthed in wonder, she peered at the
soaring animal as he flew in to drink. Now that, she
thought, is a horse worth riding.

Susan heard a 'thunk' as he landed, then the sound
of water being guzzled.

'How are you going to get near him?' whispered
Susan.

'I've got a magic bridle, remember,' hissed
Bellerophon. 'I just have to wave it and he'll come
running. Watch this!'

Bellerophon jumped up from behind the white
boulder and charged at Pegasus, waving the bridle and
shouting:

'Come to your master, horse!'

Pegasus leaped backwards, then eyed the hurtling
Bellerophon. A fraction of a second before Bellerophon
caught him, Pegasus soared into the sky. He circled
overhead, neighing and flapping his great wings.

If Susan hadn't known better she would have thought Pegasus was sticking his tongue out.

Bellerophon just stood there holding the bridle while his prey wheeled and ducked above him.

'Magic bridle, phooey!' snarled Bellerophon, hurling it to the ground and stamping his foot. 'What good's a magic bridle if he won't let me get near enough to put it on?'

Susan came out from behind the rock.

'Shouting and screaming won't do any good,' she said.

'If you're so smart *you* get him, then,' said Bellerophon.

'Certainly,' said Susan. 'I too have strong magic with me.' She put her hand in her pocket and, amidst the wadded tissue and unidentified bits and bobs, found her coin. Then, her heart pounding, she wished she were riding Pegasus.

Nothing happened.

Gritting her teeth, Susan wished again.

Zilch.

If there was anything worse than having a temperamental magic coin Susan couldn't think what it was. She had half a mind to hurl that coin into the spring and be done with it.

Bellerophon laughed.

'Some magic,' he sneered.

Blushing, she stuffed the coin back in her pocket. As she did, her fingers touched something unfamiliar.

She took it out. It was one of the sugar cubes the riding instructor had given her.

'What's that?' said Bellerophon.

'Sugar,' said Susan.

'Never heard of it,' said Bellerophon.

'Horses love it,' said Susan.

She held out her hand and walked a few paces till she was beneath the hovering Pegasus.

'Here, boy!' she called. 'Look at this.'

Pegasus circled overhead. Susan ducked as his flashing hooves passed above. His nostrils flared as he sniffed, then sniffed again.

Then he landed, several feet in front of Susan. Wings outstretched, poised for flight, he stood still, his eyes fixed on her hand.

Susan held out the sugar.

'Here boy,' she murmured, taking one step towards him. 'See what I've got for you.'

Pegasus snorted, and flew a few feet into the air.

'Come here,' coaxed Susan. She clicked her tongue the way she'd heard Eileen do.

Pegasus' nostrils twitched. He landed again, this time closer. Then slowly, delicately, he stretched out his neck and reached for the sugar. His lips felt soft on Susan's palm.

'Good boy,' said Susan. Bellerophon threw the bridle over his head. Pegasus snorted, then calmly furled his wings as he chomped.

Bellerophon leaped on his back. 'And now to fight Chimaera!' he screamed. Pegasus spread his wings and they took off.

'Hey!' shouted Susan. 'What about me?' But Pegasus and Bellerophon had already disappeared into the clouds.

Susan felt furious. The nerve of that Greek! She helps him tame Pegasus and then he flies off on an exciting adventure without so much as a thank you. And she had so wanted to ride Pegasus!

Well, that was that. What a disappointment.

Susan splashed some water on her face, then sat down by the fountain's edge and wished to be home.

At once grey mist swirled round her, but it seemed different this time. More like clouds than mist, thought Susan. The next moment she felt the wind pulling her hair while her fingers twisted round the rough long strands of a white horse's mane.

She was on Pegasus.

'How did *you* get here?' muttered Bellerophon. He was riding behind her. He looked shocked.

'Oh my goodness, I'm – FLYING!' squealed Susan. Too late she remembered her fear of heights. Her stomach lurched as she caught a brief glimpse of rocky cliffs and white-capped waves far, far below.

'Don't blame me if Chimaera incinerates you with one breath,' hissed Bellerophon. Susan didn't care. She was riding Pegasus!

'This is wonderful!' shouted Susan. 'I'm flying!'

They darted through the clouds, leaping and soaring. All too soon Bellerophon shouted in her ear:

'We'll be swooping down over Chimaera soon. I'm going to shoot her with my arrows.'

'I can help,' said Susan eagerly. 'I've done lots of archery at school.'

'Just keep out of my way,' he snapped. 'Watch out, there she is!'

Below them the monster reared up on her scaly legs and roared when she saw them. Fire poured from the lion's mouth while the dragon tail thrashed the ground.

High as she was Susan felt the heat of Chimaera's fiery breath. Pegasus shuddered. Bellerophon kicked him with his heels and tightened his hold on the bridle. Susan held tight to Pegasus' mane.

'Down!' shouted Bellerophon. Pegasus swooped low above the bellowing monster. Bellerophon took aim and shot. The arrow hit the enraged beast in the tail. Chimaera reared up and howled. A tongue of flame lashed out, catching Bellerophon's hand. There was a horrid smell of singed hair.

'Yow!' he yelped, dropping his bow as he put his burnt hand in his mouth.

Susan caught the heavy bow before it fell. Bellerophon was hunched over in pain. Then before she could stop him Pegasus wheeled about and hovered above the maddened Chimaera.

'Go, Pegasus!' screamed Susan, as Chimaera opened her jaws to release a torrent of flame. The heat was unbearable. Gripping Pegasus tightly with her knees, Susan twisted round, grabbed several arrows, then fired them again and again and again.

Chimaera writhed and sank to the earth.

Pegasus circled above, then landed gently.

Her heart pounding, Susan slid off his back. Bellerophon followed, avoiding looking at her. Ooh, her legs were sore. Cautiously, they approached Chimaera's still body. A few wisps of steam curled out of her open mouth. A single fly buzzed around her head.

Bellerophon poked the hairy, scaly body with his spear. It was dead.

'I did it!' Susan rejoiced, punching the air with her fist.

'No you didn't,' said Bellerophon sulkily. 'I gave her the death shot.'

'Didn't!'

'Did!' said Bellerophon. 'Anyway, no one would believe you. Those are *my* arrows in her.' He leaped on Pegasus' broad white back. 'I'm off to tell King Iobates the good news,' he said, digging his heels into Pegasus's flanks. The great horse unfurled his wings and took off into the sky.

'Bye, nymph!' he shouted. 'Nice knowing you!'

Susan scowled and shook her fist at him.

'Dog-face!' she shrieked. 'Deer-heart!' But Bellerophon had long since flown off.

I think he's worse than Hercules, and I didn't think that was possible, she thought. But she, at least, would always know the truth.

She took out her magic coin. A horse's head had replaced the woman's profile.

'I wish to go back to the stables,' she said, clutching the coin.

Susan felt herself falling. Down she fell, head first into a large bundle of hay. She heard a horse whinny as she spat out a mouthful and rubbed the dust from her eyes.

She was in a stable all right, but not the one she had left. This one had a chariot of ivory and gold in the corner, and only one familiar white horse.

'Hey, Pegasus,' said Susan, stroking his soft nose. 'What are you doing here?'

'Who dares speak to the king's horse?' bellowed an angry voice. 'By Hercules, you'll be fed to the hungry crows.'

It was too late to move. Susan stood still as a richly dressed man came into view. He wore a gold crown on his head and his arm glittered with bracelets. In his raised arm he held an olive-wood sceptre encrusted with gold.

'Bellerophon?' said Susan, peering at him through the gloomy light. She'd just left him not five minutes before, yet he looked so different, older, with jowly cheeks, a double chin, and greying hair.

He stared at her, then lowered his club.

'I know you,' he said slowly. 'You were with me when I killed Chimaera all those years ago. 'You have not changed, nymph,' said Bellerophon.

'When *I* killed her, you mean,' said Susan.

Bellerophon waved his hand. 'That was just the first of my exploits,' he continued. 'I beat the Amazons, defeated a band of pirates, fought off Iobates' palace guard – finally the king realized how much the gods loved me, and gave me his daughter and half his kingdom.' He sighed deeply. 'The Lycians adore me, I have a family, and all the earthly power and riches an ordinary man could desire. But frankly, it's been dull, just being a king on earth. So I thought I'd go up to Olympus and visit the gods.'

'Up to Olympus?' said Susan. Her whole body tingled at the thought. Imagine, flying up to see the palace of the gods!

'Why not?' said Bellerophon. 'Why should the gods rule over the world while I'm stuck ruling down in Lycia? I seek the higher honours I deserve. The gods have always loved me and will be delighted to welcome me amongst them, I am sure. You can come with me if you like – bring me luck.'

Suddenly Susan felt a little uneasy. He seemed awfully boastful, and from what she knew about the gods they didn't like bragging mortals. But who could pass up the chance to visit Olympus?

'Let's do it!' said Susan. Bellerophon helped her mount Pegasus, and swung himself up behind her. Then Pegasus trotted out of the stone stable and hurled himself into the sky, a whirl of white wings.

Higher and higher they rose. Susan peeked down. The land already looked tiny beneath her. Susan trembled. They dashed through the clouds, the wind whipping her hair, Pegasus' mane blowing across her eyes.

'This is too high,' she shouted into the wind.

'Wheeee!' shrieked Bellerophon. 'I'm joining the gods!'

'I'm out of here,' said Susan, closing her eyes and wishing. But the only mist swirling round her was clouds as they climbed ever higher through the mountain peaks.

Then Susan heard a harsh buzzing in her ear. Out of the corner of her eye she saw a gadfly buzz past.

What's a horse-fly doing way up here? she thought.

Suddenly Pegasus reared and bucked madly, hissing with pain. Susan clung on with all her might. But Bellerophon spun backwards and tumbled shrieking back to earth.

Susan was alone on Pegasus. She buried her face in his mane and did not look down.

Higher and higher through the clouds they flew.

Then Pegasus slowed. Susan opened her eyes a fraction and saw gigantic portals and a sparkling gate. Standing at the entrance was a wild-haired giant, blazing with light, thunderbolts clutched in his hand.

Zeus, thought Susan, shrinking down on Pegasus' back.

'Come, Pegasus, Olympus is your home now,' shouted Zeus, and the air boomed at his voice.

Then he saw Susan. He stared at her in astonishment and fury.

'What are you doing here?' bellowed the majestic god. He looked terrifying. Before Susan could answer, Zeus hurled a bolt straight at her. There was a sharp crack of thunder. Pegasus snorted and reared and this time Susan tumbled backwards. 'Home!' she screamed, falling down down down.

'Whoaa, Nellie, whooaa!'

'I don't know what got into Nellie, she's never bolted before,' said the instructor, running up and grabbing Nellie's bridle. 'You did well keeping your seat for so long, though for a moment I couldn't see you and thought you'd fallen off,' she added, looking approvingly at Susan, who sat speechless and ashen-faced on Nellie. 'I think you must be a natural rider.'

'Were you scared?' asked Eileen, bringing her pony over to them.

'Believe me,' said Susan. 'That was nothing.'

5

MINDING MEDUSA

Susan sneaked downstairs. Her parents were watching telly in the sitting room with the door open. Could she tiptoe into the kitchen and grab some sweets from the jar without being seen or heard?

Susan inched her way forward. She'd made it! She was in the kitchen! Carefully she twisted the lid off the sweet jar and grabbed a handful. Stuffing two chocolates in her mouth, she quickly tightened the lid and turned to escape.

THUNK!

Her arm knocked against the door.

Susan froze. From the sitting room came a burst of laughter. She breathed again and edged her way down the hallway towards the stairs.

Suddenly her mother appeared.

Susan shoved the remaining sweets behind her back.

Her mother frowned.

'Susan! Have you done your homework yet?'

Susan scowled.

'No.'

'Well, when are you going to do it?'

'Soon,' said Susan.

'And have you cleaned Stinky's litter tray?'

'No!'

'And tidied your room?'

'NO!' screamed Susan. 'Leave me alone!'

Her mother sighed loudly.

'I want you to go and do your work right now! Why do I always have to remind you?'

On and on her mother nagged.

'I knew this would happen!' wailed Susan. 'I should have stayed upstairs!'

Up she stomped. Wouldn't it be great to be invisible, she thought, hurling herself onto her bed? Then she could do what she wanted, and no one would bother her. That was the horrible thing about parents. Out of sight was usually out of mind. But the moment they saw you – bam! It was: 'Go to bed!' 'Stop playing on the computer!' 'Do your homework!'

Well, she'd had it.

Susan went to her drawer and got out her magic coin. She flipped it over and saw that the picture had changed. Instead of Pegasus a winged boy appeared.

Icarus, thought Susan. The boy who flew too close to the sun. She went to her bookshelf and got down her book of Greek myths. This time she'd be well prepared. She quickly read the sad story of Icarus and his father, the inventor Daedalus, their escape from their prison on Crete, and Icarus' tragic end when the wax holding his wings melted.

Now I'll know exactly what to do, thought Susan. She closed her eyes and wished.

★

'Boo hoo!'

'Boo hoo!'

Dusting herself off, Susan saw a young man sitting on the hillside beneath a flowering almond tree, hugging his knees to his face. A brightly polished shield lay beside him in the grass, sparkling in the heavy heat of the sun. In the distance were several mountains, some so tall their peaks were capped with snow. Susan heard the tinkling of bells, as an unseen shepherd ushered his flock up the steep hill track.

I don't remember this bit, thought Susan. Never mind, perhaps the story was wrong.

'Hello, Icarus,' she said, touching the young man's shoulder.

He raised teary eyes to her.

'Who?'

'Aren't you Icarus?' said Susan.

'No,' said the youth, sniffling. 'My name's Perseus.'

Perseus? What was going on?

'Just a minute,' said Susan, fishing in her pocket for the coin. There was no longer a winged boy pictured. Instead a monster's snake-covered head with bristling fangs glared up at her.

The coin had tricked her.

So much for being clever and trying to cheat, thought Susan, sighing and putting the coin away. Then she looked at the tearful young man sitting before her.

'Why are you crying?'

'Because I'm such a boastful idiot,' he moaned. 'King Polydectes, who's a miserable, horrible creep, wants to force my mother to marry him. I said no way, then he tricked me into swearing to bring him anything he wanted, and he said to bring him the head of the Gorgon Medusa.'

'So what's so hard about that?' said Susan unsympathetically.

The youth looked at her incredulously.

'First, Medusa is so hideous that anyone who looks at her is instantly turned to stone. Plus, she's protected by her two immortal winged sisters, who would catch and kill anyone who harmed her. So I'd need to be invisible *and* be able to fly away faster than they. It's impossible. King Polydectes knows Medusa will kill me like she's killed every single person who has ever ventured to the land of the Gorgons and then what will happen to my poor mother?' And he started crying again.

'Isn't anyone helping you?' said Susan.

The boy sighed. 'Well, Athena did offer me some tips,' he said. 'She told me to seek the three Grey Women and make them tell me where to find the nymphs who keep the weapons I need: a cap of invisibility, winged sandals, a pouch to put Medusa's head in, and a blade of the gods, a sword of sharpest adamant.'

'Well,' said Susan. 'That doesn't sound too hard to me. I'm the nymph, Susan, and I've helped many heroes. You seem worthy – I'll help you, too.'

'Thank you,' said the boy, wiping his eyes and perking up. 'I should warn you, the Grey Sisters are truly disgusting – they share one eye, and one tooth, and keep on the lookout for any humans they can fling into their cauldron and eat.' His face clouded over again and his lips trembled. 'Wait!' he moaned. 'How am I going to make them tell me where to find the weapons?'

'Easy,' said Susan, who had vast experience forcing Freddie to confess where he'd hidden her things. 'All we have to do is sneak up and snatch something precious of theirs and not give it back until they tell us where those nymphs are. I'd guess they'd tell you anything if you pinched their eye.'

'Eeeew, touch an ... eyeball,' choked Perseus. 'Just the thought makes me feel sick.'

'Don't be such a wimp, Perseus,' snapped Susan. 'Just think of it as wobbly jelly.'

'As what?' muttered Perseus.

'Never mind,' said Susan. 'Where do the Grey Women live?'

Perseus pointed to a nearby mountain.

'In a cave at the foot of Mount Atlas.'

'Let's go!' said Susan.

Perseus and Susan crept through the cool olive groves, stepping carefully over the nets spread below the trees, and taking care to hide themselves in case the hags should spot them. Soon they heard a high-pitched cackling.

'Where's the eye? Give me the eye!'

'No, it's still my turn!'

'No, mine!'

Peeking through the silvery foliage they saw three hideous, grey-haired women sitting at the entrance of a cave. Before them an iron cauldron bubbled. A dreadful stench rose from the pot. Susan held her nose.

'All right, here comes the eye,' said the second hag.

Perseus and Susan watched as she plucked the eye from her socket and passed it over.

'Ah, now I can see my delicious food,' sighed the third, crunching away, her filthy grey hair dangling into her bowl.

'Hurry up! Hurry up!' snapped the first.

Quietly Susan and Perseus sneaked up behind the hags as they passed the eyeball and tooth back and forth.

'Wait till the eye is in one hand waiting to be passed,' whispered Susan. 'Then sneak up and snatch it while they're all blind!'

The second one took the eye out of her socket with her clawed hand. Perseus stepped towards them.

A twig snapped.

'Quick! The eye!' shrieked the third sister. Perseus froze. His face looked pale green.

Susan leaped forward and snatched it.

Ugh! How cold and slimy and wobbly it felt!

'Where's the eye, you stupid crone?' snapped the first.

'I gave it to you, you old bag!' snapped the second.

'I have it,' announced Perseus, coming up beside Susan but refusing to take the eyeball from her. 'If you want it back, tell me where to find the nymphs who keep the weapons that can kill Medusa.'

'Never!' shrieked the hags.

'Then your eye goes straight into Lake Tritonis!' cried Perseus.

'NO!' howled the sisters.

As if he'd ever be able to touch it long enough to throw it in, thought Susan, starting to feel a little queasy herself. The grey eye in her fist wobbled about as if it were alive.

The Grey Women started howling, and then swore by the River Styx they would tell him truthfully how to find the nymphs and their magic weapons.

These were the most complicated directions Susan had ever heard. Long before they'd finished talking about journeying three days north, four days east, three days south, and back across this river and up over that mountain she was completely lost.

But Perseus nodded and smiled and thanked them.

'A curse on your thanks, you wretch,' they howled. 'Where's our eye?'

Perseus picked up a pebble and threw it at them.

'There it is!' he shouted, grabbing Susan and hurrying away, leaving the hags scrabbling over the parched ground searching and shrieking.

'What am I supposed to do with this eye?' said Susan as they ran.

'Whatever you want!' said Perseus.

I'll keep it, thought Susan, slipping it into her pocket. Then I can prove to Freddie and Eileen I've been having magic adventures. She hadn't wanted to say anything until she had proof. Now she did.

They ran until they reached the safety of an oak wood, then stopped, clutching their sides and gasping for breath.

'So, which way?' said Susan.

'Three days south,' said Perseus.

Susan frowned.

'I thought they said three days north.'

'South,' said Perseus. 'Unless it was four days north, then three days west.'

'Don't you know?' said Susan.

Perseus hesitated. 'Not really,' he said. 'I was hoping you did.'

'Oh great,' said Susan. 'Why didn't you ask them to repeat it?'

'I was too embarrassed,' said Perseus, blushing.

'What are we going to do?' said Susan.

'I don't know,' said Perseus. He looked as if he was going to burst into tears.

Susan stamped her foot. 'This is hopeless,' she wailed. 'I wish we were there right now.'

The swirling mist set them down in the midst of a glorious garden. Trees heavy with pears, pomegranates and figs stood scattered about the cool enclosure. The air was fragrant with apple blossom and sweet perfumes. A tall fountain bubbled forth in its centre, the water dripping over bright pebbles.

I don't believe this, thought Susan. She reached into her pocket and pulled out the coin, which glowed warmly in her hand. The Greek words, ΤΙ ΣΤΗΣΛΕΙΣ – what do you wish? – twinkled up at her.

I suppose the coin wants to make up for tricking

me, thought Susan. It had better be full cooperation from now on.

Then she forgot her worries, as the nymphs came out to greet them. In their hands they carried a cap, a large wallet, winged sandals, and a sharp, sickle-shaped sword.

All of these gifts they gave to Perseus. He put on the cap of invisibility, and vanished from sight. He took it off, and reappeared. He strapped on the sandals and flew into the air, somersaulting and twirling and laughing above their heads as his sharp sword sliced through the breeze.

Then Susan spoke up.

'Have you anything for me?' she asked hopefully. Wouldn't it be great to have my own cap of invisibility? she thought. Perfect for sneaking sweets and giving Eileen a good pinch without being caught!

The nymphs looked at one another.

'We have only one each of those precious things,' they said.

Susan felt bitterly disappointed.

'I see,' she said in a small voice. 'I guess that's it, then. Goodbye, Perseus,' she said, holding out her hand. 'It's been fun knowing you. Good luck killing Medusa.'

'Wait,' said Perseus. 'We could share the sandals. Here,' he added, offering her the golden wings from off his right foot. 'Put this on.'

Susan could hardly believe what she was hearing. A generous Greek hero?

With trembling hands, Susan strapped on the sandal. She suddenly felt as light as air.

'Now, take my hand,' said Perseus.

Holding hands, they flew up and wobbled above the fountain.

'Hold tight,' said Perseus. They waved to the nymphs, shouted their thanks, and flew unsteadily over the high stone wall enclosing the magic garden.

Then Perseus took off in one direction, Susan in another, and their hands pulled apart. Immediately they both wobbled and toppled backwards, flying foot first, upside down.

'Eeek,' squealed Susan.

'Catch my hand,' cried Perseus. They struggled to right themselves.

'That's better,' said Susan, hoping she'd stop feeling so dizzy soon. 'I don't think I like upside-down flying.'

'Me neither!' said Perseus. 'Now to find the land of the Gorgons!'

Over land and sea they flew, a few feet above the foamy white waves, seeking the Gorgons' lair.

Time passed, but Susan felt as if she were floating in a dream. She was almost half-asleep when Perseus squeezed her hand.

'Look.'

In the flat, rocky fields below them stood the scattered statues of men and animals. Then Susan realised that the rain-washed, petrified forms were those who had seen Medusa's terrible face.

'SSSSSSSSSSS. SSSSSSSSSSSSS.'

'Listen, Perseus,' whispered Susan.

The air was filled with the unmistakable sound of hundreds of hissing snakes.

Without a word they landed. Susan gave Perseus back the winged sandal, then he put on his cap of invisibility and vanished. Susan could feel his hand in hers, but could see nothing.

'Did you know you're invisible too?' spoke the empty air. Then his hand dropped hers. 'Not any more. Only while you're touching me.'

'Wait! Perseus!' shouted Susan. 'Come back!'

'What is it?' said the disembodied voice.

'We've forgotten something,' she said. 'Something very important. You're invisible, so Medusa can't see you. But *we* can see her.'

'Obviously,' said Perseus, reappearing before her. 'That's what being invisible means. We see them. They can't see us.'

'No need to be sarcastic, smarty-pants,' said Susan. 'That's my point. If you look at Medusa, you'll be turned to stone, invisible or not.'

'Rats,' said Perseus. 'I knew this wouldn't work.' He sat on the ground scowling.

Susan thought. There *has* to be a way round this. There has to be. She stood silently, watching the sun shining on Perseus' round shield. Her reflected face looked awfully sunburnt.

'Perseus,' said Susan. 'I know just what to do. Fly backwards.'

'So I can go crashing into those poisonous snakes and gnashing teeth? No thanks.'

'No!' said Susan. 'Use the reflection in your shield to guide you. It's polished as bright as a mirror.

'You are a genius,' beamed Perseus.

Susan smiled modestly.

'Thank you, wise hero,' she replied. 'I wish my teacher thought that.'

'Will you come and hold the shield for me?' he asked. 'I can easily carry you, and if you hold the shield that will keep both my hands free to chop off her head.'

Susan hesitated for a moment, then jumped on his back. Holding high the shield before them, they slowly flew backwards, heading towards the sounds of hissing snakes.

The terrible hulking shapes of the three Gorgons appeared in the shield. They were asleep. Huge, rasping snores burst from their fanged mouths. Their slobbery tongues lolled out into the dirt. Snakes writhed above their heads, hissing and rattling, their mouths dripping poison as their tongues poked the air.

Susan gasped. Never had she seen such frightful faces in her life. Her whole body stiffened and it took all her strength not to scream.

Slowly, cautiously, Perseus and Susan edged towards Medusa. Keeping his eyes fixed on her reflection, Perseus raised high his curved sword.

CHOP! CLUNK!

Medusa's head thudded to the ground.

Then something amazing happened.

Out of the bloody neck sprang a glowing white winged horse, which flew straight into the sky.

'Pegasus!' breathed Susan.

Beside the dead Gorgon her two immortal sisters stirred, their brass claws clenching and unclenching.

Quickly Susan held open the wallet. No way am I touching that head, she thought. I did the eye, he can do the snakes.

'Hurry!' she whispered.

Carefully, Perseus picked up the horrible head and dumped it in the pouch. The snakes, still alive, hissed and twisted. Drops of blood dripped from the bottom of the bag. As they hit the sand, each turned into a snake.

'Let's get out of here!' said Perseus. Susan jumped on his back and off they flew.

'After the murderer! Tear his flesh!' screamed enraged voices.

Susan saw the reflected, ferocious shapes of Medusa's sisters, their golden wings flapping, flying this way and that, clawing and swiping the empty air as they chased their invisible prey. Susan felt hot Gorgon breath on her neck.

Frantic to escape, Perseus suddenly lurched. Susan tumbled off and fell to the ground, knocking the breath out of her body.

'Susan!' shouted Perseus from above.

'There she is!' screeched a Gorgon.

Out of the corner of her eye, Susan caught a fleeting glimpse of a snaky face and outstretched claws as the Gorgon swooped out of the sky. Instantly, her prone body froze and a clammy coldness came over her limbs. With her last conscious breath, Susan wished.

Susan felt stiff as stone. She stared up at a ring of faces pressing in upon her. Gingerly, she tried bending a toe.

It moved.

Phew, thought Susan. That was close.

She sat up and rubbed her head. The crowd gasped and backed away, as if she were a demon.

'Zeus save us!' screamed a woman, pulling her children close to her side.

Why has the magic brought me here, she wondered, looking over a barren cliff-top into the churning dark blue sea below. She breathed in the salty smell. What was going on? Susan racked her brains to remember what happened to Perseus, but her mind was blank.

Then Susan heard the sound of tambourines.

'Make way for King Cepheus and Queen Cassiopeia!' shouted a voice.

So my adventure hasn't finished, thought Susan, gazing at the silent crowd gathered on the sea-cliff. The people parted, and amongst them walked a king and queen, clutching a young girl who stood beside them in chains, surrounded by armed spear-carriers. Susan pushed her way forward to get a better view.

'Oh! Woe is me!' howled the queen.

'Woe is me!' shrieked the king.

'Woe is me!' howled the queen even louder.

'Woe is *me*!' squealed their daughter. 'I'm the one who's to be sacrificed to a sea monster! And it's all your fault, Mum!'

'All right, I might be a bit to blame,' snivelled the queen. 'I did say I was more beautiful than the sea nymphs, which is the truth, but I've been punished for my plain-speaking, haven't I?'

'Ha!' shrieked the girl. '*You've* been punished!'

'You know perfectly well Poseidon, blue-haired Sea Lord, sent a sea serpent against us, and the prophets said we had to sacrifice you, Andromeda,' said the queen, weeping. 'If the prophets had said me I would gladly take your place.'

'The gods have sent a stranger among us!' shouted a woman's voice in the crowd. 'A stranger who appeared from nowhere!'

Rough hands pushed Susan forward.

Queen Cassiopeia whispered to her husband. A smile spread across his lined face and he nodded.

'What's going on?' said Susan, as soldiers seized her.

'Surely, husband, this girl is a gift from the gods,' exulted the Queen. 'Why should we sacrifice our lovely Andromeda when this stranger will do just as well?'

'Good thinking, wife!' said the king.

'Now wait a minute!' shouted Susan. 'I am the nymph Susan! You can't do this! The gods will punish you!'

No one paid the slightest attention. Susan was hustled along a steep cliff-track almost down to the narrow stony beach. Someone tore off her jeans and shirt and a long white tunic was placed over her head. Then a soldier gathered up her clothes and pitched them into the sea.

'NO!' screamed Susan. 'My coin!'

On the furthest rock jutting out above the frothing water was a small ledge. Susan fought and struggled, but there were too many soldiers. They left her chained to the rocky cliff, the waves lapping at her feet.

Susan tugged frantically at her chains. It was no use. She was fastened tight against the cliff, her feet barely supported by the narrow ledge. Below her, well out of reach, her jeans and shirt bobbed in the shining water, gradually drifting further and further out to sea. Looking up she saw King Cepheus and Queen Cassiopeia shielding their eyes against the sun as they peered anxiously towards the horizon. Andromeda had her hands covering her ears. The only sound was the harsh cries of the sea birds.

Stay calm, thought Susan. Stay calm. This is bad, in fact it's very bad, in fact it's terrible, but I'm going to keep my head. She breathed deeply, and tried to think.

Then Susan saw a far-off shape rising up from the wine-dark sea. She strained against her irons. It wasn't a ship. It wasn't a whale. And whatever it was, it was speeding straight at her.

'HELP!' screamed Susan.

A giant set of fins sliced through the water. A pronged tail lashed the foam, sending waves crashing against the rock and splattering Susan with spray. A giant serpent's head, dripping with slime, leered at her out of the foam, its hideous green body coiling and uncoiling.

'HELP!' screamed Susan. 'HELP!'

The sea monster was so close she could see its blood red spiked tongue, and rows and rows of sharp teeth.

The monster came closer, its slavering jaws wide open ... Susan shut her eyes.

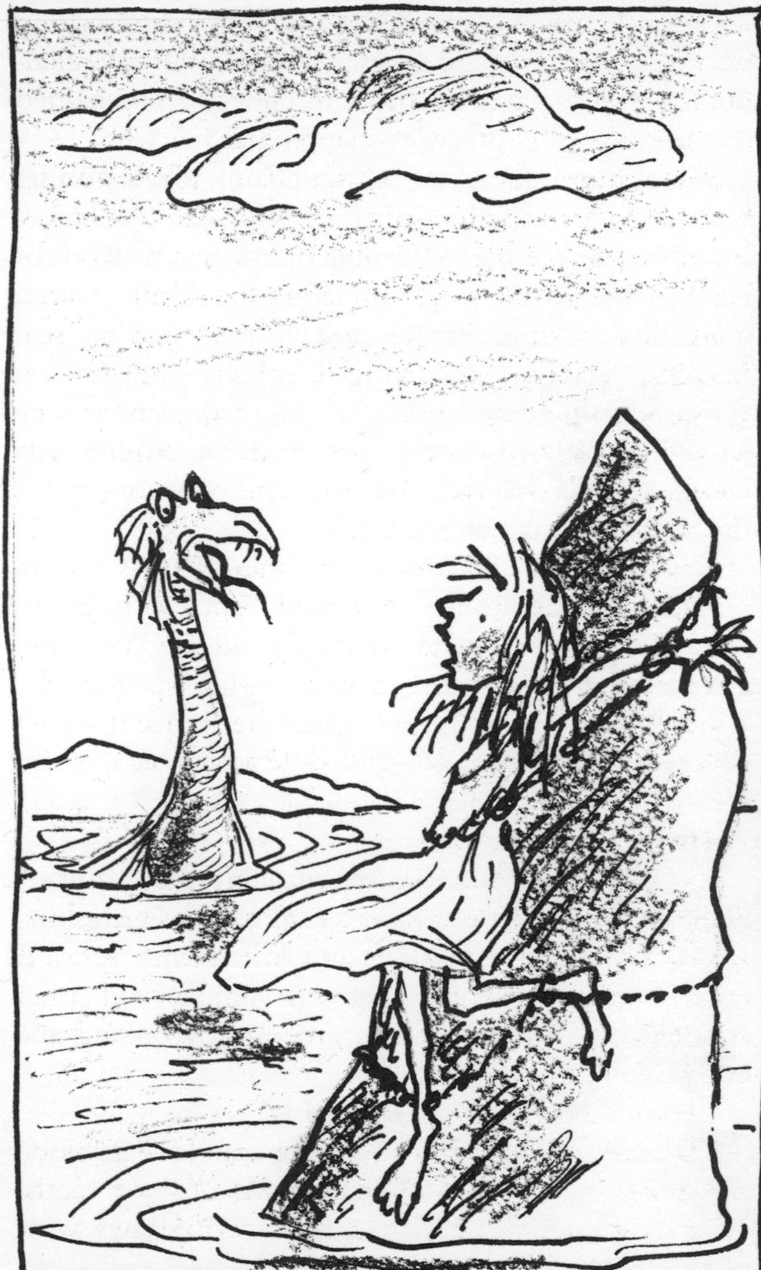

'Hey, what is this?' hissed a hoarse, gutteral voice. 'This isn't Andromeda. I was promised Andromeda. No way am I eating this.'

Susan opened her eyes.

The monstrous snake was so close she could have reached out and touched it.

'And what's wrong with me?' she demanded hotly, without thinking.

The serpent belched. Bones spewed from its mouth and plopped into the sea.

'I only eat the best,' it hissed. 'You're too small and freckly and sunburnt – uggh. I like princess, not pipsqueak. Give me Andromeda – OR I'LL CRUSH YOU ALL!' it bellowed, suddenly rearing up to its full monstrous height.

The people cowering on the clifftop fled, screaming. 'Sacrifice Andromeda!' they shouted. 'Give Andromeda to the monster!'

'FOOD!' boomed the serpent. 'I want food!'

It shook its fearsome head.

'Maybe a little snack first,' it hissed. 'Just to whet my appetite.'

Uh oh, thought Susan, shrinking against the cliff.

But the sea snake turned and plunged into the water, chasing after a dark bobbing shape.

Susan willed the bobbing thing, whatever it was, to escape. But the monster was too fast. Swiftly overtaking, it gulped and swallowed. Then the sea snake wheeled round and zoomed back for shore. Suddenly it stopped. A strange expression came over its cruel face.

'Bleeeech!' it choked, spewing something from its mouth.

SPLAT!

Susan's sodden, smelly clothes smacked against her face as the heaving monster plunged underwater.

Soldiers unbound her, chaining the screaming, struggling, weeping Andromeda in her place on the rocky cliff. Then everyone scuttled away to safety as fast as they could.

'Get out of here while you can!' one soldier shouted to Susan as he ran off.

Susan snatched up her slime-covered clothes and turned to follow. Her hand fumbled in her pocket. The coin was safe. Susan felt so happy she could have danced.

'Help me!' screamed Andromeda as the sea snake's fins sliced through the foam.

'HELP!'

Susan hesitated. How could she leave Andromeda chained? Yet what could she do? If only she had Medusa's head, she could turn the monster to stone!

'Oh, I wish Perseus were here!' she cried.

There was a whirr of wings and Perseus swooped out of the sky, hovering above the waves with the heavy wallet slung over his shoulder. He looked a little bewildered.

'Ah Susan,' he said, shaking his head. 'Thank the gods you escaped from the Gorgons! What's going on? Why is this girl chained here? What are you −'

Suddenly the monster reared up behind him, its mouth open.

There was no time to lose.

'Watch your back!' shouted Susan. 'Turn the monster to stone!'

Perseus, bless him, did not hesitate or ask stupid questions, thought Susan approvingly, as the youth leaped into the air, yanked Medusa's head from out of

the bag and held it before the sea monster.

The snake froze into stone, its ridged back curving down to the water.

'Hurray!' shouted Susan.

Then Perseus drew his sickle sword of adamant and sliced through Andromeda's chains. The girl fell weeping upon him.

'Good work, Perseus,' said Susan, jumping up and down with excitement. 'Let's go and climb on that serpent!'

But Perseus ignored her. He was whispering to Andromeda, and she only had eyes for him.

Susan snorted.

Oh no, love stuff, she thought, sighing.

She certainly did not want to hang about for *that*.

Susan closed her eyes and wished to be home.

'Susan! Have you done your homework?'

'NO!' she howled back.

Some things never changed.

6

MIMICKING
MIDAS

'If you could have any wish, what would you wish?' asked Susan, lounging outside one sunny summer afternoon in the hammock.

'I'd wish for all the chocolates in the sweet jar,' said Freddie promptly, squashing his sandcastle. 'And a hamster.'

'That's two wishes,' said Susan.

Eileen looked up from her book.

'Naturally I'd wish for all the wishes in the world,' said Eileen.

'That's generally considered a greedy wish,' said Susan. 'Bad things always happen to people who wish that. Just like people who wish to live for ever and forget to say they'd like to be young for ever and end up grizzled old grasshoppers.'

'Oh yeah?' snapped Eileen, without lifting her eyes off the page, 'and what would you wish then, if you're so smart?'

Susan swung back and forth in the hammock.

'I'd wish,' she said, 'that everything I touched would

become better than it was. So this hammock would have beautiful embroidery, my clothes would turn to silk and my school dinners would taste delicious.'

Eileen didn't look at her.

'That's not completely stupid,' she said, grudgingly. 'Too bad you'll never got the chance to wish it.'

'I wouldn't be so sure about that!' Susan replied.

Eileen stopped pretending to read.

'And what exactly do you mean by that?'

'I've got a magic coin,' said Susan recklessly. 'I can travel back to Ancient Greece.'

'Liar!'

'Am not!'

'Are too!'

'I am not lying!' shouted Susan. 'I have got a magic coin. And I've helped loads of heroes like Hercules, and Perseus, and that nincompoop, Paris.'

Eileen turned up her lip.

'You are the biggest liar I ever met.'

'I can prove it,' said Susan.

'Go on then,' said Eileen.

Susan reached into her pocket. Now where was that eye? Her fingers fumbled into every corner. There was a jelly-like smear but no eye.

'I had the eye of the Grey Women but it must have dissolved,' said Susan regretfully. She would have liked to have seen Eileen's horrified face.

'Oh yeah, right,' sniggered Eileen.

'Okay then,' said Susan. She took the coin from her pocket. It sparkled and glittered as if it had turned to gold. 'Come with me and I'll prove it.'

Eileen rolled her eyes.

'Come on.'

Freddie stepped out of the sandpit and obediently grasped her hand.

Eileen stood irresolute.

'What have you got to lose?' said Susan.

Eileen lightly touched one of Susan's fingers.

'Oh this is stupid,' she exclaimed, dropping Susan's hand, as Susan wished.

'OUCH!'

'OUCH!' shouted Freddie, even louder. 'I'm being prickled!'

Gingerly, Susan disentangled the thorny rose bush from Freddie's sandy leg.

'Smell those roses, Freddie,' said Susan, to distract him from his scratches. The scent of roses was over-powering: the warm air was heavy with their sweet fragrance, and the hum of bees and wasps.

She looked around at the magnificent walled garden. There were roses stretching in every direction, great lush bushes heavy with flowers, a maze of pinks and reds and whites.

So many roses, thought Susan. Have we landed in some garden show by mistake?

'Is this magic?' said Freddie.

'Just stick with me and be quiet,' said Susan, sweating in the heat and already regretting that she'd brought along a five-year-old on a magic adventure. He was sure to be a nuisance and start whining just when things were getting exciting.

A man ran towards them, his long violet cloak flapping about his knees, wearing a flat, wide-brimmed wool hat. Three slaves, wearing short tunics, ran behind.

'Daughter! Son! The most miraculous news!' he shouted.

'That's not daddy!' said Freddie.

'Just pretend it is!' whispered Susan back. 'We're playing pretend.'

'Okay,' said Freddie, nodding vigorously.

The man came closer, gasping for breath. 'I found this old satyr drunk in the garden,' he panted, 'and I looked after him. Turns out he was the teacher of the god Dionysus! To reward me, Dionysus has granted me one wish! Hurray for me! Three cheers for King Midas!'

'Wish for lots of chocolate,' said Freddie.

King Midas paused. His eyes gleamed.

'What's chocolate?' said Midas. 'Some rare jewel?'

'No,' said Freddie, 'you eat it. He's not very clever, is he Susan?' he added in a loud whisper.

'Shh!' hissed Susan. 'I know a great wish,' she said eagerly. 'Wish that–'

'Quiet, you stupid children!' interrupted Midas. 'I was born to be rich! When I was a baby a procession of ants carried grains of wheat up the sides of my cradle and placed them between my lips – the prophets said this was a sure sign I would be wealthy beyond all dreams! And now I have the perfect wish! I want everything I touch to turn to gold!'

'I'm sure that's not wise,' said Susan quickly.

'And why not?' demanded Midas.

'Because–' Susan hesitated. What *was* wrong with that wish?

'Well, who cares what you think?' said Midas rudely. He shouted:

'I want to be rich! I want to be filthy rich! I wish everything I touch to turn to gold!'

'Are you sure?' boomed a voice from the sky.

'Sure I'm sure!' shouted Midas. Then he looked down at his clothes. Everything he wore glittered gold.

He stooped and picked up a pebble.

Gold.

He touched a rose.

Gold.

He touched a tree.

Gold. Even the dun-coloured earth beneath his feet turned yellow as he capered.

'Yippee!' shouted Midas. 'I'm rich.' He flung his arms around a vine. Gold grapes hung from the trailing gold branches.

Freddie ambled over to a heavy golden rose. It broke off in his hand.

'Have it, boy!' shouted Midas. 'There's lots more where that came from!'

'What do you say, Freddie?' prompted Susan.

'Please/thank you,' said Freddie, tucking the gilded rose safely into the pocket of his shorts.

Why shouldn't I have some gold, too? thought Susan, stooping and filling her pockets with golden pebbles. They felt very heavy.

Midas clapped his hands.

'Slaves! Bring me food! All this gold is making me hungry!'

At once servants appeared carrying a table. Others followed, holding ivy-wood bowls of sloshing wine, roast meat, and round loaves of bread. One of the slaves carefully diluted the wine with water, then poured the drink into rich goblets.

Midas pulled up a chair – which turned to gold – tore off a hunk of bread, and put it in his mouth.

CLANG!

'Ouch!' shrieked Midas, clutching his cheek. 'Bleeeeech!' He spat out the gold morsel and grabbed a hunk of meat.

CLANG!

'Son, pass me some wine!' he commanded.

Freddie inched forward and carefully picked up a brimming vessel. Midas snatched it from him and poured the liquid down his throat.

CHOKE!

'AAAAARGGH!' shrieked Midas, leaping up and pushing Freddie aside. 'I'm HUNGRY!'

'NO!' shouted Susan, as a golden Freddie toppled over and lay still, a fallen gold statue.

'Don't touch me!' shrieked Susan, putting out her hands.

But she was too late.

Before she could pull away, Midas' fingers brushed her shoulder. At once Susan's body stiffened. She stood, frozen to the spot, gleaming gold from head to toe.

Susan was so angry she would have stamped her foot, but she could not move so much as a golden eyelash. All she could do was stand there. She could hear Midas cursing and yelping and begging the gods to take away his dreadful wish. Then he ran inside his palace, slamming the golden door.

This is boring, thought Susan.

This is very boring, she thought, some time later.

THIS IS EXTREMELY BORING! she fumed. I always did hate playing musical statues. And being a real statue is even worse. I'd wish to go home but what to do about Freddie? I can't just leave him.

Gradually Susan's thoughts petered out. The light faded, and she felt herself drifting into a frozen state where time stood still.

SPLASH!

Susan's face felt wet. Gasping and spluttering, she felt her stiff body return to life.

'Thank goodness that worked!' said King Midas, standing before her holding an empty jug. 'Dionysus said I should wash in the river Pactolus to get rid of that cursed wish. Now the sands are gold, but mercifully you're not.'

'I'm soaking wet!' said Susan. Her whole body tingled as the blood suddenly flowed again in her veins. Freddie sat up, shaking his wet head.

'Susan, I want to go home,' said Freddie, tugging on her sleeve. 'I've got pins and needles everywhere.'

'Just a little longer,' said Susan. She turned to Midas. 'How could you have wasted that wish?' she demanded.

King Midas hung his head.

'All right, I admit it, I was a ninny,' said King Midas.

'Ninny!' squealed Susan, rubbing her stiff arms and legs. 'Total dimwit you mean! Why didn't you listen to me? I could have told you the best wishes.'

King Midas sighed.

'You're right, of course,' he said. 'Next time I'll know better. Now cheer up and come along, both of you, we don't want to miss the music contest. My old friend the woodland god Pan has challenged the god Apollo to a music competition. That's no contest – Pan is the greatest!'

'I want to go home,' said Freddie stubbornly.

'Nonsense,' said Midas. 'Wait till you hear Pan's lovely music.'

'I don't want to hear lovely music!' screamed Freddie.

'How about a piggy-back ride there?' said King Midas, scooping Freddie onto his back and galloping off. Freddie squealed with laughter.

He just wants to distract us from how silly he's been, thought Susan, as she hurried after them into the forest.

Soon she found herself in a grove of gnarled olive trees, their silvery leaves rustling in the breeze, near the bottom of a sloping hillside. A crowd had gathered round the edges. In the centre of the grove was an empty armchair, covered in creamy ram skins. Beside the chair a tall, stony-faced young man paced up and down, his forehead wreathed with laurel, holding a lyre made from a gleaming tortoise shell. Nearby pranced a strange, hairy, bearded creature, half-man, half-goat, with horns jutting from his forehead.

'Pan!' shouted Midas.

The satyr came bounding up to Midas.

'You're sure to win, Pan,' said Midas. 'Your pipes can outplay Apollo's lyre any day.'

'*I* certainly think so,' boasted Pan.

'My daughter is quite an expert on the Pan pipes,' boasted Midas.

I am? thought Susan.

'And her lyre playing – oooh la la!' said Midas, kissing his fingers.

'This I must hear,' said Apollo coldly.

'Really I couldn't,' said Susan, backing off.

'Play,' said Apollo, offering her his lyre.

'I'd love to but I can't,' said Susan. 'I hurt my hand playing basketball – I mean, weaving baskets.'

'But your lips are working fine,' said Apollo, snatching Pan's pipes from him and forcing them into Susan's hand.

'I haven't practised for ages,' said Susan. 'I'm not – '

'PLAY!' ordered Apollo. 'Or I'll turn you into a tree.'

Susan brought the pipes to her lips.

'Wrong end,' muttered Pan.

'Oops,' said Susan. She hastily turned them round. Apollo sniggered.

Then, puffing up her cheeks, Susan blew.

'Plllllughhhhhh,' groaned the pipes.

'Plllllughhhhh! Peep! Plllgh! Peep!'

Apollo grimaced.

Susan flushed bright red and handed the pipes back to Pan.

'I'm a little rusty,' she murmured.

'Wasn't she great!' beamed Midas. 'My daughter the genius!'

Susan was so embarrassed she wanted to run

away. Real parents were bad enough without being humiliated by fake ones.

A cry went up.

'Here comes the judge!'

An ancient old man, dripping with leaves, was helped into the chair. Trees followed him, nodding when he nodded, moving when he moved, swaying when he swayed.

'That's the judge, the old mountain god Tmolus,' whispered Midas.

'Are you all right, Tmolus?' asked Midas. 'Not too cold for you?'

Tmolus cupped his ear.

'Eh?' squeaked Tmolus.

'ARE YOU COMFORTABLE SITTING THERE?' shouted Midas.

'I am not spitting!' shouted Tmolus.

'Have you travelled far?' asked Midas.

'What jar?' shouted Tmolus. 'Stop spouting nonsense.'

'*He's* the judge?' whispered Susan.

'EH?' said Tmolus. 'Let the contest begin!' The forest shook as he spoke.

Pan picked up his pipes.

A wild, eerie, frightening sound poured from his reeds.

Wow, thought Susan, swaying her shoulders. Freddie danced about to the spooky music, pounding and stamping. With a final flourish of fast notes, Pan finished.

Midas cheered. Susan clapped. Freddie whistled.

Everyone else was silent.

'Bravo! Bravo! Encore! Encore!' Midas whooped. 'Now that's what I call music, right, judge?'

'Eh?' said Tmolus.

Then Apollo stood. His long purple robes swept the ground. His top lip curled in a sneer as his left hand swept up the lyre. Then he began to play.

TWANG A-TWANG A-TWANG. The slow, stately melody, Susan thought, was haunting. But so depressing! She stole a look at the audience. Everyone looked utterly miserable.

Freddie tugged at her sleeve.

'I need a wee,' he said.

'Shh,' said Susan.

Freddie tugged harder.

'I NEED A WEEWEE!' he insisted loudly.

There was a sudden, terrible silence.

Apollo paused, his fingers poised over the strings.

'What mortal dares interrupt the playing of the god of music?' he demanded.

'I need a wee,' said Freddie stubbornly. 'Where's the loo?'

Apollo's face was dark with rage.

'How dare you?' he spat.

'Freddie!' hissed Susan. 'There aren't any toilets here! Go behind a tree.' If she could have made the earth swallow her up she would have done.

'By Hercules,' said King Midas, going up to Apollo, 'when a boy's gotta go, he's gotta go. Come along, son,' he added, steering Freddie behind a gnarled olive tree circled by a rough stone wall.

Pan gave a loud laugh. No one dared speak.

'I will begin again,' said Apollo frostily as Freddie returned, his shorts twisted about his waist. 'The next mortal who so much as breathes will be turned into an onion.'

'I don't like onions,' whispered Freddie.

'SHHH!' hissed Susan.

When Apollo finished playing his dirge, everyone except King Midas clapped and cheered. He stood instead, arms folded. Then he gave a loud yawn.

'Boring!' shouted Midas.

Tmolus awoke with a start.

'Apollo is the winner,' he said.

'Boo!' shrieked Midas. 'Unfair! Pan was much better.'

'The judge was asleep,' protested Susan.

Slowly Apollo turned and stared down at Susan and King Midas. His face was flushed.

'Did someone speak?' he asked coldly.

'I did,' said Susan. 'You played beautifully but you have to admit this contest was unfair.'

'Not fair,' said Freddie.

'Pan is best, Pan is best,' chanted Midas.

'Shh,' hissed Susan.

'But he *was* better,' insisted Freddie.

Apollo fixed them all with an angry stare.

'Perhaps you are having trouble with your hearing?' said Apollo.

'I don't think so,' said Susan.

'My ears are excellent too,' said King Midas.

'I just had my hearing test,' said Freddie.

Apollo pointed his finger at them.

'Let me help make your ears even better,' he hissed.

BOING! BOING!

Susan grabbed her ears. They were sprouting under her hands. Taller and taller, furrier and furrier they grew.

'Ha ha, Susan, you look so funny!' shrieked Freddie, laughing and pointing. 'Susan's got donkey ears, Susan's got donkey ears.'

'So have you, Freddie,' snarled Susan.

'Help! Help!' shouted Midas, trying to hide his huge ears under his hat.

'Mummy!' squealed Freddie.

Susan decided enough was enough.

She grabbed Freddie's hand, and wished.

Eileen blinked.

'So? I'm waiting,' she said.

'We've been gone for ages,' said Susan. Just in case, her hands covered her ears. 'Freddie and I were with King Midas.'

'Yeah! I got turned into a statue and everything,' said Freddie. 'And Susan has donkey ears!'

Eileen sighed.

'Well, she doesn't now,' said Eileen.

What a relief, thought Susan. She didn't fancy wearing a hat for the rest of her life.

'We have proof,' said Susan. 'Gold! Go on Freddie, show her your gold rose.'

Susan took out of her pocket a handful of ordinary pebbles, while Freddie stared as the faded pink petals crumpled to dust in his hand.

'Ha!' said Eileen.

7

HORRIFYING HERCULES

A camping holiday! It had sounded such fun when Mum and Dad suggested it. What they hadn't said was that it would mean sharing a tent with her brother and sister, and hot muggy weather and endless long hikes where Susan would have to lug her own backpack. Freddie naturally got to carry a tiny pack with some sweets in it, and Susan was sure that Eileen's pack was much lighter than hers. They'd just been out on what Mum called a midnight hike, but which was really just a night-time walk around nine p.m. – big deal. Finally they were back, and everyone was asleep. Everyone but Susan.

Susan lay hot and sweaty and uncomfortable in the tent. How she hated sleeping bags! What was the point of lying on stony ground in a damp old bag that smelled of cats when you could be tucked up snug at home in your cool, comfy bed? Plus the sound of Eileen snoring, and Freddie muttering, was enough to stop anyone sleeping.

Oh, I wish I were somewhere cool, thought Susan,

yawning, her outstretched hand touching the jeans she'd tossed onto the ground.

Susan blinked. Was she asleep? One moment she was in a hot, humid tent, the next sitting on a grassy mountain slope. She breathed deeply.

Ah, fresh mountain air! Susan stood and gazed at the tall peaks all around her. She was on the highest of all, and still nowhere near the top, which was so high it was shrouded in mist. It feels as if I could touch the sky, she thought, raising her arms in happiness. Then she noticed her clothes. Or, rather, her lack of them.

Oh dear, thought Susan, I'm only wearing my nightgown. But come to think of it, no one had ever seemed bothered by her clothes, and her long night-

dress looked a lot more like a flowing Greek tunic than jeans, that's for sure. Susan decided not to worry.

What a glorious view! Wasn't life grand? She inhaled, filling her lungs with the sweet smell of cypress trees. Wait a minute. What was that stench?

The horrid, stinky smell of sweaty fur suddenly filled Susan's nostrils.

'Pooh!' she said, waving her hand in front of her face.

'YOU!' groaned a grumpy, oddly familiar voice. Susan turned round.

'YOU! Oh no!'

Of all the Greek heroes, she *would* have to meet that double-crossing no-good Hercules again, still wearing that smelly old yellow lion skin tied round his waist, still carrying that same grubby olive-wood club. Doubtless still all brawn, and no brain.

'I certainly hoped I'd seen the back of you, girly,' said Hercules, looking disgusted. He was sitting in the shade of a cypress tree. 'Things are hard enough for me without having you in the way.'

'As I recall,' snapped Susan, 'I was very useful to you cleaning those stables. You'd still be there shovelling if I hadn't come up with my brilliant plan. For which, incidentally, you never thanked me.'

'I don't remember,' said Hercules, looking sulky.

'Well, I do,' said Susan.

'Well, I don't,' said Hercules.

Susan decided to let bygones be bygones and change the subject.

'What labour are you on now?'

'The twelfth and final one,' said Hercules, sighing.

'So why don't you get on with it instead of sitting

here like a great big lummox?' said Susan harshly. It
was harder to let bygones be bygones than she'd
thought.

'Because I don't know how to proceed,' said
Hercules. 'This is the hardest one yet, and I've had
some toughies, including grabbing Cerberus from
Hades–'

'Oh, that sweet old pooch,' said Susan, waving her
hands dismissively. 'He's just a big softie, really. I tamed
him with Orpheus, you know.'

Hercules rolled his eyes. 'We'll see what Orpheus
has to say about that.'

'Go ahead, ask him,' said Susan.

'I certainly will,' said Hercules.

They glared at each other. He was just as awful as
ever, thought Susan. She decided not to waste another
second in his company.

'I'm off,' she said. 'Goodbye, good luck,' and good riddance, she thought, heading down the mountain track. She'd have a nice stroll before going home.

'Wait,' said Hercules.

'Why should I?' snapped Susan. She did not turn round.

'I – need – your – help.' Hercules spoke as if the words had been torn out of his mouth with hot pincers.

With difficulty, Susan stopped herself from gloating.

'All right,' she said. 'What's this new labour all about?'

'I have to bring that dog-face, Eurystheus, three golden apples from the garden of the Hesperides, which is somewhere here on the slopes of Mount Atlas.'

'What's so hard about yanking a few apples off a tree?' said Susan.

Hercules looked as if he would have liked to yank her off the mountain.

'Oh, just the small matter that Ladon, a hundred-headed dragon who never sleeps, is curled round the sacred tree trunk,' he said. 'Plus the tiny detail that no mortal can enter the garden. Oh, and did I mention that the Titan, Atlas, who holds the sky on his shoulders, built high, impenetrable walls around it, to protect his daughters, the nymphs who tend the garden. Other than that, it's a piece of cake.'

'No need to be sarcastic,' said Susan. 'What's your plan?'

'Bash the walls down and take my chance with Ladon,' said Hercules dolefully.

Susan shook her head. 'It's always smash bash crash

with you, Hercules,' she said disapprovingly. 'Why not simply ask the nymphs to give you the apples?'

'Why should they? The daughters of evening tend the apples for Hera, the queen of heaven. Plus I can't get into the garden to ask them, can I?'

'Can't you get someone else to fetch the apples for you? An immortal who knows the nymphs?'

'Like who?'

Susan thought. 'What about this Atlas then? Couldn't he fetch the apples for you?'

Hercules gave a short laugh.

'Oh sure. You've forgotten something. He supports the heavens on his shoulders. The sky would fall and crush the world if he left this mountain.'

Susan looked carefully at the giant before her. She had a crazy thought.

'Why don't you switch places with him?' she asked. 'That is, if you're strong enough to hold up the sky?'

Hercules puffed out his gigantic chest.

'I'm strong enough for anything,' he boomed.

'Then ask him,' said Susan.

Hercules looked at her. A slow smile spread across his face.

'I like that plan,' he said. 'I'd rather hold up the heavens than face that dragon. Let's go.'

'But I'm not wearing climbing shoes,' protested Susan.

Hercules scooped her under his arm as if she were a feather. Then he started walking quickly up the winding mountain path.

Up and up and up they climbed, till they were lost in the swirling mist hiding the mountain's summit.

'Atlas stands at the very top,' panted Hercules.

'I hope we're there soon,' said Susan. 'I don't like being carried like a sack of potatoes.'

'Sack of what?' said Hercules.

'Olives, olives,' said Susan.

Then she heard a vague, indistinct moan. The higher they climbed, the clearer the words.

'Oh, my aching back! Oooh, my poor shoulders!' mumbled the voice.

'Atlas! Yoo hoo! Atlas!' shouted Hercules.

'Who comes here to the ends of the earth?' boomed a voice from high up in the clouds.

Looming before her, Susan saw a giant, as tall as a mountain. He was stooping forward, and on his massive shoulders rested the pale blue sky.

Hercules plonked Susan down, none too gently.

'Oy, watch it!' she complained.

'It's me, Hercules,' he said. 'I've come to ask a favour. Will you fetch me three golden apples from the garden of the Hesperides, and I will hold up the sky until you return.'

A look of disbelief, followed by absolute joy, spread over the giant's sunburnt face.

'I would love to stretch my legs again,' said the Titan. 'I will gladly do this errand for you.'

'Great,' said Hercules. 'Thank you.'

'No, thank you,' said Atlas.

'No, no, thank *you*,' said Hercules.

'Glad everyone's happy,' said Susan quickly, afraid she'd have to listen to them thanking each other all day.

'Brace yourself and I will pass you my great burden,' said Atlas. Then he shrugged the sky onto Hercules' head and shoulders.

Hercules shuddered. For a moment Susan feared his legs would buckle under the colossal weight. Then he steadied himself. That was close, thought Susan, suddenly realising that if Hercules faltered the sky would have crushed her.

'Oof,' groaned Hercules, his back bending and swaying with the great weight of the heavens. 'That's heavy.'

'You're telling me,' said Atlas, straightening up with a gigantic CR-EEEAK! 'Now don't go away,' he added, chuckling, 'I'll be back very soon with those apples.'

Off he went.

Susan sighed and sat down.

'I suppose we just wait now,' she said.

'Ooh, my shoulders,' complained Hercules. 'Let me see if I can get more comfortable.'

He hoisted the heavens up a bit onto his left shoulder. The sky tilted alarmingly.

'Whooa!' shrieked Susan. 'Straighten up! The sky is falling!'

Hercules jerked the sky a little higher onto his right. The sky sloshed to the left.

'Steady on!' cried Susan.

The sky lurched and wobbled.

Hercules lurched and wobbled.

'Watch out!' said Susan, trying to prop him up.

The sky straightened.

'Careful!' said Susan.

'You have no idea what it's like holding the sky on your shoulders,' grumbled Hercules. 'And I'm getting sunburn on my neck, I can feel it.'

'Sorry,' said Susan. 'Shall I help you hold?'

Hercules glared at her.

'Be my guest,' he snapped. 'Your holding a cloud
will make all the difference.'

'Okay, I won't then,' said Susan. 'Anyhow, I'm sure
Atlas will be back any minute.'

Slowly the day turned to night. Still Atlas did not
return. The first stars twinkled in the dark heavens.
They hung so low Susan tried to reach up and touch
them. She stood on tiptoes, but they sparkled just out
of her reach.

'Do you think he's coming back?' said Hercules.
He'd been silent for hours.

'Of course he will,' said Susan. But she had been
worried about the same thing. Would Atlas seize his
chance of freedom and never return? Then Hercules
would be trapped here for ever, and it would be all her
fault.

'My head is itchy,' complained Hercules.

'Maybe you've got nits,' said Susan. 'Everyone at my school keeps getting–'

'It's the stars, stupid. I never realised how pointy they were. Ouch! Oooh! Eeek!'

THUD! THUD! THUD!

'Atlas!' shouted Hercules, as the giant loomed up out of the darkness. 'Thank goodness you're back.'

Phew, thought Susan. For a while she'd thought they were in big trouble.

Atlas lumbered into view, the three golden apples glowing like suns in his hand.

'Hercules, I've been thinking,' he said. 'I'll deliver these apples to Eurystheus for you. I can walk a lot faster than you can, and if you'll just hold the heavens for a few more months I'll be back as soon as I've completed this labour for you.'

Susan stood up sharply. He'll never come back, she thought. Hercules will be trapped here for ever. Even slow-witted Hercules could smell a rat.

'It's an awfully long journey to Tiryns,' said Hercules, frowning. 'I'd hate to inconvenience you.'

'No trouble at all,' said Atlas, smiling. 'I've been standing in this same spot for thousands of years. Do me good to stretch my legs. Cheerio.' And Atlas set off into the night at a jaunty pace.

'Now what are we going to do, smarty-pants?' hissed Hercules. 'You and your great ideas.'

'I'm thinking, I'm thinking,' hissed Susan fiercely. How did she try to make Freddie do something he didn't want to do?

'Oh, Atlas,' called Susan.

'Yes?' said the Titan, reluctantly turning around.

'I think that's a super plan,' said Susan. 'If anyone

deserves a holiday you do. And my friend Hercules here is really enjoying the glory of holding up the heavens – you will tell everyone about his great feat, won't you?'

'Certainly,' said Atlas, smiling.

'There's just one thing. As you know, the stars are awfully ticklish. If you would just take back the sky for a moment, while Hercules gets a pad for his head, it would make everything much more comfortable for him.'

'Good idea,' said Atlas. He nodded, and laid down the apples.

'Now watch how I do this,' he said. Slowly and carefully, he stooped and eased the awful burden of the heavens off Hercules' aching shoulders.

'See,' he said. 'You balance the weight evenly, like this. Much easier.'

Hercules rubbed his back and slowly straightened his weary body. Then he scooped up the apples.

'You know, Atlas,' he said, juggling the golden globes in his giant hand, 'you hold the heavens so much better than I do. I think perhaps I'd better take the apples to Eurystheus after all.'

And with that, Hercules and Susan hastened off, leaving Atlas moaning and cursing behind.

'Poor Atlas,' said Susan. 'I feel bad for tricking him.'

'I don't,' said Hercules. 'It is his fate to hold the heavens.'

Susan suddenly felt very tired.

'Well, I'm off,' said Susan. 'Soon you'll be a free man again.'

'Thank you for your help,' said Hercules suddenly. 'I am grateful.'

'You're welcome,' said Susan, smiling. 'And now I wish to go home.'

Nothing happened.

Silly coin, she thought, reaching into her pocket. Except that she didn't have a pocket. Her hand slid down her nightgown. Susan stood absolutely still. She had a sudden flash of memory, of her hand brushing against her jeans as they lay on the ground. The full horror of her predicament hit her. She was trapped in Ancient Greece, while the magic coin lay in a tent in the twenty-first century.

For a long moment Susan could not breathe. Then her heart began to pound.

'Oh my-' gasped Susan. She clasped her hand to her mouth. 'The coin! It's back home with my sister and brother! Hercules! Help me! Help me!' And Susan started to scream. A terrible howling yelp of terror burst from her throat.

'I will call to them,' said Hercules.

'I will call to them,' said Perseus, joining him.

'I will call to them,' said Andromeda.

'I will call to them,' said Orpheus.

They formed a circle round her.

'It's no use,' said Susan tearfully. 'Eileen and Freddie are too far away to hear. HELP! HELP!' She screamed despite herself, because she could not swallow her fear.

The four Greeks stood silent. They cupped their hands to their open mouths, but no sound came out.

'See?' said Susan, starting to cry again. 'I told you there was no point.'

Two small shapes walked out of the night mist towards her. Both wore pyjamas. One rubbed his eyes. The other looked as if she were sleep-walking.

'This is not happening,' said Eileen. 'This is not happening.'

Susan thought she had never seen such a beautiful sight in her life as her sleepy brother and dazed sister. She hugged them both so tightly that Freddie squealed to be let go.

'What are you doing here? How did you know?'

'We heard people calling,' said Freddie. 'I'm not sure what happened next.'

'Oh thank you, thank you,' said Susan, turning around. But the heroes had vanished. How on earth had they managed to summon her family?

'This is a dream,' said Eileen. 'I am having a waking dream. It's quite common, really. I'm asleep in the tent. Sound, sound asleep.'

Freddie gave Susan the coin. It felt thin and smooth, as if it were worn out with the mighty magic it had just worked. Susan gripped the hands of her brother and sister, and wished.

They were back. Back in the hot, stuffy, smelly, wonderful tent.

Freddie and Eileen sank down onto their pillows and fell instantly back to sleep. Susan was too shaken by what had happened to even lie down. Instead, she unzipped the tent flap and stepped outside.

It was a gorgeous moonlit night. And the stars! It looked as if the whole sky was covered in pinpricks of light. Susan gazed at the stars and constellations which twinkled and sparkled and took shape before her eyes. There was Orion, with his belt of three stars. There was Perseus, Andromeda, and Pegasus. And Orpheus' lyre. And there was Hercules.

'Susan! Susan! Susan!'

Susan spun round. The voices were everywhere, calling to her from the stars.

'Thank you, Susan! Thank you!'
The air reverberated with their echoing sound.
Susan flung out her arms.
'No!' she cried. 'Thank you.'

HELP!

I was once discussing my favourite characters from Greek myths with some friends. I mentioned the monster 'Shimmerer', the goddess 'Athen', the god 'Possedon'. No idea who I'm talking about? Neither did my friends. I meant to say 'Chimaera', 'Athena', and 'Poseidon', but I didn't have a clue how to pronounce them correctly. Here's the guide I wish I'd had.

ALPHEUS al-fay-uss

ANDROMEDA an-drom-med-a

APOLLO a-poll-oh

APHRODITE aff-ro-die-tee

ARISTAEUS ar-iss-tay-uss

ATHENA ath-ee-nah

ATLAS at-lass

AUGEAS ow-gay-ass

BELLEROPHON bell-air-oh-fon

CASSIOPEIA cass-ee-oh-pee-ah

CEPHEUS sef-ee-uss

CERBERUS er-ber-uss

CHIMAERA kim-air-ah

CORINTH corr-inth

CRETE creet

DAEDALUS dy-dall-uss

DIONYSUS dy-oh-ny-suss

ELIS el-liss

ERIS air-iss

ERYMANTHIAN er-imm-an-thian

EURYDICE you-rid-ee-see

EURYSTHEUS you-riss-thee-oos

GORGON gore-gone

HADES hay-deez

HERA hair-a

HERCULES her-kue-leez

HERMES her-meez

HESPERIDES hess-**perr**-id-eez

ICARUS ick-er-uss

IDA eye-da

IOBATES eye-oh-**bah**-teez

LADON lah-donn

LYCIA liss-ee-ah

MEDUSA med-**yoos**-ah

MENELAUS men-ay-**lay**-uss

MIDAS my-dass

OENONE ee-**noh**-nee

OLYMPUS oh-**limp**-uss

ORION oh-**rye**-on

ORPHEUS or-fee-uss

PACTOLUS pack-**toe**-lus

PAN pan

PARIS par-iss

PEGASUS peg-a-suss

PELEUS pee-lee-uss

PERSEPHONE per-**sef**-oh-nee

PERSEUS per-see-us

PIRENE py-**ree**-nee

POLYDECTES poll-ee-**deck**-teez

POSEIDON po-**sy**-don

PYTHIA pith-ee-ah

SATYR sat-er

SISYPHUS siss-ee-fuss

SPARTA spar-ter

STYX sticks

TAENARUM tee-**nare**-rum

TANTALUS tan-ta-luss

THETIS thee-tiss

THRACE thrayss

TIRYNS tirr-inz

TITAN tie-tan

TMOLUS t'mole-uss

TRITONIS try-**toe**-niss

TROY troy

ZEUS zee-ooss

Also by Francesca Simon

Horrid Henry
Horrid Henry and the Secret Club
Horrid Henry Tricks the Tooth Fairy
Horrid Henry's Nits
Horrid Henry Gets Rich Quick
Horrid Henry's Haunted House
Horrid Henry and the Mummy's Curse
Horrid Henry's Revenge
Horrid Henry and the Bogey Babysitter
Horrid Henry's Stinkbomb

Big Class, Little Class

and for younger readers

Don't Be Horrid, Henry
Illustrated by Kevin McAleenan

Miaow Miaow Bow Wow
Moo Baa Baa Quack
Illustrated by Emily Bolam